MASKS

Lydia was familiar with the golden death masks of the ancient Greeks—but she was an innocent in a world of modern masks and deadly deception.

Mrs. Erskine, the charming and eccentric dowager ... Bubi, the plump and amusing German film producer ... Mary-Lou, the ravishing and featherbrained young actress ... Annie Ollenshaw, her short-spoken companion ... Henry, the smooth-talking and witty writer ... Major Papandros, the elaborately polite Greek official ... Marius Blunt, the strangely secretive archeologist ...

Too late Lydia discovered none of them were what they seemed ... too late to avoid the net that had been woven for her ... too late to escape the sinister terror that claimed her ...

THE
YELLOW
GOLD OF
TIRYNS

✠✠✠✠✠✠✠✠✠✠✠✠✠✠✠✠✠✠✠✠✠✠✠✠✠✠

HELENA OSBORNE

A DELL BOOK

Published by
DELL PUBLISHING CO., INC.
750 Third Avenue
New York, New York 10017

Printed in the U.S.A.
First Dell printing—March 1971

THE
YELLOW
GOLD OF
TIRYNS

❖❖❖❖❖❖❖❖❖❖❖❖❖❖❖❖❖❖❖❖❖❖❖❖❖❖❖❖❖❖❖

Nicos said, "There is your hotel!" and the car drew up in a scrunch of gravel at the very edge of the quay. Half a mile away, clearly reflected in the dazzling sea surrounding it, a gray fort seemed to float, becalmed.

Lydia and Mrs. Erskine climbed out stiffly and stood gazing at it, shading their eyes.

"Honey," said Mrs. Erskine reverently, "I had just no idea that Greek temples were going to be as beautiful as that."

"It's not exactly a temple," Lydia said carefully. "It's a Venetian fort, I think. About three hundred years old."

"Nothing to do with the Greeks then?"

"Not with the *ancient* Greeks . . ."

"Oh, my," Mrs. Erskine sighed humbly. "What a lot you're going to have to tell me."

Lydia smiled at her with affection. "Nonsense!" she said, with more conviction than she felt. "You're making giant strides."

"I never learned any of it," Mrs. Erskine had said, "and I'm too old now to try getting Greek history out of books. You'll just have to treat me like one of your girls. Around fourth grade, I'd say, not bright but willing to learn." At the time it had seemed a fairly straightforward proposition—Lydia had been teaching Greek history to the upper sixth for more than five years now and could do it in her sleep. But the upper sixth had at least been through the lower sixth; Mrs. Erskine seemed to be virgin soil.

Now Mrs. Erskine said proudly, "But I remember you said there *was* an old Greek place just near here. Terry something, was it?"

"Tiryns. Yes, that's perfectly true. Very interesting." Lydia was disconcerted to hear her voice dropping into its classroom tone.

"So where's that?" Mrs. Erskine sounded challenging.

"I don't know, I'm afraid." Lydia glanced around apologetically, as though a Mycenaean citadel might be lurking unnoticed. But only the white houses of Nauplia crowded down to the edge of the quay.

"Well, then," said Mrs. Erskine with one of those lightning changes of direction that Lydia, after an acquaintanceship of only two days, still found disconcerting, "let's have lunch. Mr. Nicos!"

Nicos, who had been gazing with satisfaction at the island, now turned around to be congratulated. "So you like my island?"

"It *belongs* to you, Mr. Nicos?"

"Not exactly." Nicos was only slightly deprecatory. "But I find it for you, no? Miz Erskine—" He took her elbow in a confidential grip. "The manager at the hotel is my friend. He will look after you. When you see him, you will say to him, 'Nicos the driver tells me to come to you.' No? You will say—"

But Mrs. Erskine had got the idea by now and detached herself politely. "Right now," she said clearly, "we need lunch."

"I will telephone to the island," Nicos cried with enthusiasm. "For a boat. You wait."

"But how long will that take?"

"Quarter hour. Perhaps half. No trouble. You wait."

"But I'm *hungry*." Mrs. Erskine was suddenly plaintive. "I don't think I can wait that long. How about you, Lydia?"

"Food would be very nice." They had left Athens at ten, and breakfast seemed to have happened in another world.

"Isn't there somewhere we could eat right here?"

"There is the Belle France," said Nicos doubtfully, indicating a large untidy building just along the quay. "But I do not think . . ." Clearly the manager at the Belle France was not his friend.

But Mrs. Erskine had taken in the solid-looking chairs and tables scattered on the gravel outside the hotel, and she set off without a further word. Choosing a table with a good view of the island, she sank down with a little sigh of contentment. "Here, Mr. Nicos," she said, pulling out a chair as he and Lydia caught up with her, "come and sit by me."

But Nicos looked uncomfortable. "Please excuse me," he said. "Is not good lunch here. I show you another restaurant in the town? The manager . . ."

But Mrs. Erskine only smiled and shook her head, and finally, with a fat bow, he disappeared, disconsolate, around the corner of the hotel.

There was a moment of complete silence, and then Mrs. Erskine and Lydia spoke at once.

"I guess," said Mrs. Erskine, chuckling, "I just struck a blow for individual liberty."

And Lydia murmured, chiefly to herself, "Greece. At last. The wine-dark sea . . ."

It's not a chance that anyone turns down lightly— Greece for three weeks in April with all expenses paid and a generous salary thrown in. If you're a junior school mistress in Cirencester who until three months ago had a widowed mother to support and care for, you don't even hesitate, but you may have the most terrible misgivings. Mrs. Erskine's niceness had been a bonus, an uncovenanted mercy. They had met only the previous morning, when Lydia was shown into the big comfortable suite at Claridge's. Mrs. Erskine had been sitting very straight on the sofa, her perfectly manicured hands clasped in her lap and every gray-blue hair in place. She radiated wealth, and Lydia had felt suddenly sure that all her worst apprehensions were about to become fact. But then Mrs. Erskine had spoken.

"Oh, Miss Barnett!" she had cried, jumping to her feet and smiling up into Lydia's face as they shook hands. "How nice to see you, and what a wonderful surprise! I've been so terrified of meeting you. They wrote me that you'd been to college and were a schoolteacher and all, and I was so afraid you'd be severe and elderly, and here you are so pretty and young and nice-looking and I'm so *relieved!*"

It was a disarming introduction, and Lydia was duly disarmed. Smiling at Mrs. Erskine as they sat down, she saw in the big mirror over the fireplace a tall girl in green, with long legs and a pointed face under smooth, dark hair, leaning back in a corner of the sofa and looking—yes, it was true—extremely pretty. *Kind Mrs. Erskine*, thought Lydia. *Clever Mrs. Erskine.*

"Now, I want us to have a *good* time on this trip." Mrs.

Erskine was off on another tack. "We won't kill ourselves sight-seeing, but when we do go anywhere you'll tell me what we're looking at and *why*, and then I won't feel so lost as I generally do when I'm up against *history*. It's terrible to be so stupid about these things. Lucky girl!" She had changed direction again. "Blue eyes and dark hair. My daughter had just your coloring."

Had? Lydia didn't say it, but Mrs. Erskine saw her face.

"Oh, no!" she exclaimed and laughed. "It's just she's rather gray now. There." She pointed to the mantelpiece. "I've never been away from them before, and I know I'll miss them all so much."

In the center of the row of photographs was a nice-looking woman of about thirty-five with a boy and a girl, both rather fat and teenish.

"That's several years ago, of course. This is Janie now, last December, on her twenty-first." A single string of pearls, a soulful expression and far too much hair.

"But Janie is—"

"My granddaughter. My daughter's eldest. I haven't a more recent one of Jane herself, though."

"But you can't have a granddaughter of twenty-one!"

"Oh, but I can!" Mrs. Erskine was delighted. "I married Mr. Erskine when I was only nineteen, you see. This is Bobbie, my son"—a square, Nordic face and smooth hair—"and this is Mr. Erskine . . ." Horn-rimmed spectacles and a bald dome. She paused. "Mr. Erskine doesn't really *enjoy* foreign travel. . . . Well, now, that's my family. I miss them terribly already. But you and I are going to have a wonderful time—I'll probably forget all about them! Now." She sat down on the sofa again. "I want to ask you what you think. I'd like to start with a few days very quiet—and you must be exhausted if school only let out yesterday. The travel agent says there's a pretty spot by the sea, not far from Athens, where we could rest up for a few days and sit in the sun and just get used to being there. And there's no museums or sights or *anything*. Would you like that?" Mrs. Erskine's views on sight-seeing—and *history*—were becoming clearer every moment.

"It sounds lovely," Lydia said, repressing her disappointment.

"I've got the name in here somewhere. There's a hotel

on an island." Mrs. Erskine extracted a neat notebook and a pair of spectacles from her enormous handbag. "Nauplia."

"Nauplia!"

"You know it?"

"Well, no. But I know about it. It *is* lovely, I believe. But it's also just beside several of the most exciting places."

"Exciting?"

"Well, most interesting historically."

"Which are those?"

"There's Mycenae and Tiryns and Asiné. All very early."

"Temples and things?"

"No, not temples. Castles, really . . . old cities. It's all rather before temples."

"*Before?* But I thought temples were terribly old."

"Well, yes. Fourth and fifth century mainly."

"B.C.?"

"Yes."

"And these other places are before that?"

"About fifteenth."

"*Fifteenth* B.C.?"

"Well, yes. They're really prehistoric sites. All we know about them is from things that have been dug up. There are marvelous things, I believe, in the museum at Athens."

"I think it's just wonderful of you to know all this."

Lydia froze. But there had been no irony in Mrs. Erskine's voice, only genuine admiration.

"Is this what you studied at college?"

"Well, yes. But I've been reading guidebooks. I've always wanted to go to Greece."

"That's nice. Me too. So you'd like to go to Nauplia?"

"Oh, yes."

"Well, then, that's settled. Good. Now let's have some coffee. Will you ring that bell? Oh, this is going to be so *nice.*"

It certainly is, Lydia had thought, reaching for the bell. In fact it all seemed wonderfully improbable—though that in itself was unlikely in a job arranged at short notice through the International Congress of Women Graduates.

They had flown to Athens that same evening and had been met at the airport by the fatly smiling Nicos with an enormous elderly Buick. He had taken charge at once, whisking them through customs and sweeping them off through the warm darkness, never drawing breath but pouring out a flood of information about ancient and modern Greece, drawing their attention relentlessly to anything that could remotely be classed as a *sight*. "American cemetery. Very many. Nightclubs. Let's twist again, cha cha cha! . . . Feex . . . feex. Very good." They flashed past the factory making Fix beer. "Somehow you see . . . now . . . yes! Acropolis!" And there it had been, brilliantly lighted, floating improbably above the lights and shadows of the city, tantalizingly half-concealed by tall buildings and by the twists and turns of the elderly Buick that Nicos directed more like a yacht tacking against the wind than a car making its way in a stream of traffic.

Lydia had longed to stay in Athens, but Mrs. Erskine had been adamant. "There'll be time enough for all that later," she had said. "Right now it's a rest I need." And after a night in the sort of hotel that Lydia had previously seen only in films, they had set off for Nauplia through a countryside of vivid and astonishing greenness. Everywhere along the road were fields of olive trees, and between them, on every scrap of stony ground, the dramatic green of young corn. Among the corn but lower, nearer the ground, were tiny yellow flowers showing only as a wash of color among the green stalks. And every now and then there had been the crimson splash of poppies.

Lydia, who had expected a tawny, rather barren countryside, could hardly believe her eyes.

"I had no idea Greece was ever as green as this."

"I expect we've caught it at just the right moment," Mrs. Erskine said. "The prairie's like this for a few weeks." She looked around her at the amazing blueness of air and sea and laughed. "No, not like this, of course. But it gets very green for a while before it all dries out again."

Twenty miles out of Athens the road had climbed steeply to run for a while along the cliff top. From that height the whole gulf of Salamis had been visible, the sea below them a vivid turquoise streaked with a darker blue where the wind struck it. In places it was dead flat, hard-looking, reflecting the trees on the farther shore. And beyond, farther to the south, were the hills of the Peloponnese.

At Corinth there had been an extraordinary moment

when the car passed over a broad metal bridge and, glancing down, they had seen a great rift—a straight, even cut that might have been made with a knife—and right at the bottom of it the narrow ribbon of sea. Then they were up into the hills again, the road twisting and curving and the fields full of little trees covered with white blossoms. Farther on, where the road rose higher and there were no more fields, there were beehives scattered through the hills in groups of twenty or thirty—little square packing cases painted a tired and dusty blue.

And then, at last, the road had started to run downhill again, and they had come out of a narrow valley to find themselves looking down a long slope of hillside to a wide plain and to the sea beyond. The hills were still rocky and barren, but the plain was checkered in bright green and brown, with occasional squares of a paler, dusty green where the olive plantations were. Nicos had gestured over toward the left. "Mycenae," he had said proudly.

Lydia had looked eagerly, but there was nothing to see except a sloping hillside and, beyond, a bare gray spur of rock running down from the hills into the plain.

Then they had passed through Argos, a bustling modern town, and had emerged onto a road leading across the coastal plain to Nauplia. Mile after mile of orange plantations surrounded them, the even lines of dark green bushes opening and closing rhythmically, like the pages of an enormous book, as the car swept past.

Now, exhausted by the impact of new sights and impressions, they were glad to sit silent in the hot sunshine —barely thinking, even—watching the fort, which floated in the center of the bay with the low dark hills of the Peloponnese in the distance beyond it.

There weren't many other lunchers. Three dark-suited Greek gentlemen at the next table were eating with concentration, and four, evidently American, ladies in sensible shoes were arguing over the menu. But Lydia's attention was fixed at once by the couple sitting near the edge of the quay. The girl had a soft baby face, deeply tanned, huge eyes made still more enormous by unabashed makeup and a squashy mouth painted a pale, improbable pink. Her fine hair fell straight to her shoulders, bleached to an ash-blond so pale as to be almost white. She was wearing loose pink silk trousers and a lime-green shirt that left her golden midriff bare. She was startlingly lovely, but it wasn't only her looks and her clothes; there was something leisured and deliberate about her movements —an expectation of cameras—that said unmistakably "model."

When Lydia caught sight of her, she was leaning back in her chair, motionless, her long silken legs gracefully extended. It was not a face intended by nature for the expression of thought—or even of emotion. But there was no doubt that just at that moment she was thoroughly cross. Lydia would have expected the man beside such a vision to be attentive and eager, but he too was slouched in his chair, staring out to sea with his hands in his pockets. Lydia couldn't see his face, but his shoulders were eloquent of boredom.

"My!" breathed Mrs. Erskine beside her. "Just look at those pants. Do you think—"

A ravishing smell distracted her. The waiter had appeared with two large plates—sardines, anchovies, tomatoes, olives . . .

"So good." It was a sigh of pure contentment. "But what's that?" Mrs. Erskine poked with her fork. "With *suckers* on?" Horizons were widening all around.

Afterward there was broiled fish, golden and delicious, and salad. Mrs. Erskine, sniffing dubiously at the wine, said, "It smells to me like face lotion."

"I think I like it," said Lydia slowly. It was cold and harsh, with the smell of pines and a color like sunlight.

"Well, if it's the thing—I guess I can learn to like it."

Greek history or retsina, thought Lydia sleepily, sipping her wine, *Mrs. Erskine will fight it on the beaches, she will fight it on the airfields, she will never surrender . . .*

"Excuse me, I am so sorry."

Lydia glanced up. One of the dark-suited Greek gentlemen was standing by their table. As she looked, he bowed briefly, clicking together his highly polished heels.

"Excuse me," he said again. "It is very stupid of me, but I have no matches and I wondered whether . . ."

"Oh, of course." Mrs. Erskine leaned sideways to pick up her enormous handbag. "I'm sure I have some someplace."

"How kind," he said, his eyes not moving from Lydia. His face was deeply lined, and his hair, cut short, was iron-gray; but the eyes were black and shining, and his whole person was charged with energy and decision.

"I heard you speaking English." He gave a quick smile that creased the corners of his eyes.

Mrs. Erskine, rummaging in the labyrinths of her handbag, gave a laugh of sincere amusement. "You didn't hear *me* speaking English!"

"Ah! You are American?"

"Yes, that's right, quite a different language, and—"

Lydia watched the man curiously. It was the most blatant attempt to scrape acquaintance, the oldest and most transparent device of them all. And yet his whole manner belied his words and actions. For all his easy insinuating chat, he remained detached and ultracorrect. Lydia knew that he wouldn't sit down with them even if they asked him—he didn't *want* to. He just wanted a few words with them. Why?

Suddenly he addressed Lydia directly, so that she was obliged to answer. "And is this your first visit to Greece?"

"Yes," she said reluctantly.

"Do you like it?"

"Yes, I do." He listened intently to her replies, but as though listening to her voice rather than to what she said. His own English was fluent and only lightly accented.

"And your mother—"

Mrs. Erskine laughed again, this time with the beginnings of irritation. "Miss Barnett's not my daughter—we're just friends. Here, keep the box." Her voice was suddenly dismissive. Lydia was impressed; the man was left with no choice but to bow again and return to his friends.

"You've made a conquest," Mrs. Erskine said easily, settling herself more comfortably in her chair.

"No, I don't think so." *One can always tell if one has . . .*

"Oxford now." Mrs. Erskine's thoughts had moved on in an orderly progression. "Was that nice?"

"Oh, yes. Yes, Oxford was marvelous."

"Lots of beaux?"

"Bows?"

"Admirers, boyfriends."

"Oh, yes, some."

Six years ago was a lifetime.

"Nobody special?"

"No, nobody special." Just the long succession of delicious, romantic friendships. Copies of Herrick and Marvell stained with river water or scattered with butter from the crumpets. *Let us roll all our strength and all our sweetness up into one ball,* they had read aloud fervently, tripping slightly on the difficult consonants. But they hadn't meant it, and neither had she. It had all been a charade. A long succession of delicious charades of love that had flowered as dazzlingly as the chestnuts along the riverbank, and faded as gently. *All so long ago,* thought Lydia sadly, reaching for the wine again. *All so long . . .*

"Oh, look!" Out of the golden haze of the wine a boat had appeared, a tall white yacht sliding across the flat blueness of the bay. A shimmering, insubstantial boat, an imaginary boat, *that gently, o'er a perfumed sea, the weary wayworn wanderer bore. . . .* Faintly across the water came the reverberation of engines. It was real all right.

"What a beauty" said Lydia softly.

"Isn't she lovely?" Another figure had stopped beside their table. "Made by the Italians, of course. No one else can produce a hull like that." This time it was unmistakably an Englishman. "Here, waiter! I want to pay. Pay. Bill. *Conto.*" He gestured energetically.

There was a drift of lime green behind him. So this was the man who had been looking out to sea—but transformed now, galvanized.

"She was made for an Italian millionaire, but he went for a private jet instead. Silly ass."

He was short and solid, with an honest, shiny face and brown hair. He was gazing out at the yacht now, his face alive with enthusiasm. "She's the loveliest thing. *Arcady.* Thank God she's back." He turned back to them apologetically. "I'm so sorry to butt in, but I was pleased to hear you admire her."

"Does she belong to you?" Mrs. Erskine asked with interest.

"Er, no. But I—we—belong to her. At least—"

The sound of the engines died suddenly. There was complete silence. The young man whipped around and gazed out at the yacht again.

"Oh, my God. Now they're anchoring instead of bringing her up to the quay. That means an hour's delay with the customs. At the very least." He drooped.

"Why don't you sit down and have a cup of coffee with us?" Mrs. Erskine was sympathetic.

"May I really? How very kind. Oh." He remembered the goddess behind him.

"Both of you," said Mrs. Erskine graciously.

There was a pulling up of chairs.

"My name is Henry James," he began. "Now please don't say anything." Mrs. Erskine looked puzzled. She hadn't thought of saying anything. "And this is Marianne Louisa Anderson. Just call her Mary-Lou."

Mrs. Erskine introduced herself and Lydia. The goddess nodded and produced a little smile.

"You said you belonged to the yacht?" prompted Mrs. Erskine.

"Well, yes." He struggled with a hip pocket and extracted a wallet. Mrs. Erskine examined with respect a visiting card reading: ARCADIA PRODUCTIONS INC., LOS ANGELES. GEORGE S. BENEDICT, DIRECTOR. In tiny print in the bottom left-hand corner was: *Public Relations, Henry James*.

"Movies?"

"That's right."

"But how exciting!"

"How does the yacht come into it?" Lydia asked. "Are you making the film here?"

"Just location shots. Not that we've done very much yet. Terrible trouble with the cameramen. And something to do with Greek equity."

"And—er—Mary-Lou?"

"Oh, yes. She's in it. Making her film day-boo, aren't you, love?"

The goddess spoke.

"Double-crossing bastard," she said distinctly. Lydia was startled. For some reason, perhaps because of Henry James' own impeccable accents, she had been assuming that Mary-Lou was English. But the voice came from the deepest south of the southern United States.

To fill what seemed likely to be a nasty pause, Lydia said quickly, "And is it an interesting job, Mr. James?"

The young man had appeared not even to hear Mary-

Lou's intervention. Now he said, almost shyly, "Oh, please, you must call me Henry. I mean, please do. In the film world, everyone's on first-name terms, and I'm just not used to 'Mr. James.' No, it's not interesting. There aren't any public relations. They just use me as a nanny for *this*—" He indicated Mary-Lou with a movement of his head. "They go off to shoot background stuff in the islands and don't need her along, so they leave her here and leave me with her. Well, I ask you! I came with *Arcady* —that's the yacht—I mean, I came because of her, because she's so marvelous, and I certainly didn't reckon on this."

Lydia braced herself for the inevitable but now, she felt, richly merited riposte from Mary-Lou. It never came. Indeed, Mary-Lou seemed to accept Henry's account of his duties quite without rancor. She even produced the little smile again.

"Where the hell are those customs men? They ought to be out to her by now." Henry had turned around on his chair and was looking at a large building far down the quay. They could just see that three men were standing together in front of the door.

Suddenly he produced from the pocket of his jacket a large, businesslike telescope which he snapped open and focused on the customs building.

"Just talking. Always talking. God, these wops." He clicked the telescope shut.

"No one can leave the ship or go out to her till they've been. But do they care? And it's not as if they didn't know her—we've been here nearly a month."

He swiveled on his chair again and, reopening the telescope, trained it on the yacht, twisting the lens slowly until the focus was right.

"Ah, there she is. What a honey . . . what a treat. Would you like to look?" Politely he offered the glass to Lydia.

Sea, rather misty and blurred; the fort, incredibly clear, with a girl in a black dress leaning over the stone wall of a wide balcony; and then, suddenly, the yacht, exquisite, motionless, and absurdly close. The name *Arcady* was clearly visible, in dark blue lettering on the white bows. A man wearing shorts and a bright checked shirt was lying in a long chair on the deck, and as Lydia watched, a woman appeared from inside the yacht and stood talking to him, gesturing energetically from time to time. She was tall and slender, but it was too far away to see her face. After a few moments Lydia swung the glass around, looking at the hills, the bushy trees on the bay shore reflected in the glassy water, an old man mending nets on the edge of the quay. Suddenly a familiar figure sprang into view, enormous, blurred but recognizable.

"Goodness," said Lydia. "There's Nicos."

She lowered the glass. They could see him now, walking briskly toward them along the quay.

"Who's Nicos?" asked Henry.

"Our driver."

"He can't have spent much time on lunch," said Mrs. Erskine.

"You have a car of your own then?" Henry asked with interest.

"Rented," said Mrs. Erskine briefly.

"Oh, I see. Are you here for long?"

"We have no settled dates," said Mrs. Erskine firmly. "This is a *real* holiday. Lydia, I think I'd like to get out to the hotel now."

The waiter had appeared beside them. "I have telephoned for the boat, madam." He seemed to know all about them.

"Oh, are you staying on the island?" said Henry. "It's called the Bourtzi, you know. You'll like that. They've hardly touched it. But there's plumbing and things. All very comfy. Well, I do hope I'll see you again. We're all staying here." He indicated the Belle France. "I'm generally around."

"Don't you stay on the boat?"

"Lord, no." He laughed. "The customs are in such a state about the Adelmann finds they wouldn't let you leave a chimpanzee on board overnight. Not a male one anyway."

"What—" started Lydia, but Nicos was beside them and Mrs. Erskine was shaking hands with Mary-Lou and Henry and moving off toward the edge of the quay.

"Good-bye, Mary-Lou," said Lydia reluctantly. "Good-bye, Henry."

"Good-bye, Lydia," said Henry. "Have a nice time."

TWO

A large open motorboat was tied up to the quay, its engine running, their suitcases already neatly stowed. Nicos helped them both in and stepped back onto the quay.

"When you want me, just ask at the Belle France. They will find me."

"Oh, thank you, Mr. Nicos. Not till tomorrow anyway. Probably sometime in the morning."

"Bye-bye, then. Good sleep!"

The tall boy who had been sitting in the stern raced the engine, and the boat swung around and headed out toward the island.

"You know," shouted Mrs. Erskine over the noise of the engines, "I'm being *terribly selfish*. I didn't ask if you wanted to come out to the hotel now. I was just feeling so sleepy after all that kerosene and I wanted a nap. But if you'd like to stay on shore and look at the town or anything . . ."

They had a clear view of Nauplia now, piled up above its quays. A huge gray castle was balanced precariously on the top of the rocky headland behind the town, and in the sunlight it all looked southern and delicious—blues and pinks and whites, with the dark shadow of trees in between. Lydia looked at her watch. It was still only just after three, and she didn't feel in the least bit sleepy.

"Well, you know, I *would* rather like that."

"Or you could go to one of your prehistoric places—if you wouldn't mind going again when you take me."

"Oh, they're all miles away, I think. But are you sure—"

"Yes, of course, dear. Take the car if you can find that Nicos—or just take the car. I don't suppose he'd mind."

They were quite near the island now. Three young girls in black dresses with broad white collars were standing on the jetty. When the boat stopped, they helped Mrs. Erskine out and two of them scampered on ahead into the fort with the luggage.

"Why don't you take the boat right back?" said Mrs. Erskine. "And just suit yourself about this evening. I'm going to take a nap and unpack and then write letters, so I won't expect you till dinnertime."

"All right. If you're really sure." Lydia turned back to the tall boy. "I'm sorry, but I'd like to go back to the shore again. Right away."

His eyebrows rose, but he climbed obediently back into the boat.

"You're very kind," Lydia said to Mrs. Erskine.

"Nonsense. Have a nice time, dear." Mrs. Erskine waved as the boat backed away from the jetty. "See you at dinner."

"Good-bye. Have a nice siesta."

Chugging back toward the shore, Lydia opened the guidebook and looked for Nauplia. The first sentence she saw was: "Tiryns lies only three kilometers from Nauplia, just beside the road to Athens." Three kilometers! But that was less than two miles . . . and Tiryns of all the places was the one she most wanted to see. Nauplia would have to wait.

The car was still parked on the edge of the quay, but Nicos had disappeared. Lydia moved hesitantly toward the Belle France. The lunchers had all finished and the tables were deserted. There was no one about, not even a waiter. She glanced in at the door of the hotel, but there was no sign of Nicos. He's probably gone to have a sleep, she thought. She couldn't possibly wake him up and ask to be driven two miles. A hundred yards away across the square four stalwart figures were climbing into a blue bus marked ATHENS. Lydia recognized the American ladies who had lunched at the Belle France. She broke into a run.

"Could you possibly take me just as far as Tiryns?" The driver, welcoming the ladies aboard, shrugged. The bus was only half full.

"Okay."

Less than five minutes later, "That's it," he said, stopping the bus briefly and gesturing with his head toward a mound among the orange plantations.

Stepping down into the road, Lydia felt a great slide of anticlimax. She had been thinking of Mycenaean "fortresses" and "palaces," and Tiryns was only a low, grassy hump. As the bus roared away along the road toward Athens, she started walking slowly, almost reluctantly, down the narrow track—and as she approached the long flat mass of the ruins, it seemed to heave itself out of the ground and rise higher and higher until it towered above her.

An enormous wall hung over the path, huge blocks of tawny stone fitted together like the cells of a honeycomb. *The walls of Tiryns were built by the Cyclops.* Pausanias had said that. Pausanias, the first of the tourists, the forerunner of the ladies in sensible shoes. And the walls must have looked very much the same in the second century after Christ, thought Lydia, as they do now: bleak and fierce and terrifying. Who could blame him for believing they weren't built by human hands?

She paid the attendant and started to thread her way through the ruins. Almost at once she found a broad paved path, a wide ramp leading upward by easy stages between high walls. Halfway up there had been a gateway, and there were holes where the metal hinges had fitted into the stone.

The shape of the doorway and the position of the hinges were so familiar, so modern, that they seemed incongruous among the vast jumbled walls. But the sense of recognition was illusory, thought Lydia—or, rather, misleading, because it brought one no nearer at all to the people who had made the hinges or cut the stone. She could see quite clearly the heavy wooden gate studded with bronze swinging back to let a chariot through, and the sweating horses, slipping and clattering on the steep slope. But the driver of the chariot, braced against the jolting of the bronze wheels, and the man who tugged the great door open—their faces were blanks, and when they spoke to each other it was impossible to imagine what they were saying. And yet, perhaps the charioteer too would have looked familiar, modern, incongruous—with a bald head and a smile of tolerant amusement . . .

For Lydia had managed to make one visit during her time in Athens: before they had set out that morning she had gone to the museum. And in the first big hall she had come face to face with a dead man—unmistakably dead, and yet at the same time fully conscious and even amused. It was a jovial face, with protuberant eyes and thick, well-shaped eyebrows below a high and shiny forehead; the face of a man who has seen and done much and can now, in tranquillity, take a detached pleasure in observing human folly. Considering, Lydia had thought, that it may well be the face of a man who was murdered on his first night home from the war, by the wife of the leader whom for ten years he had faithfully followed and served, the expression of tolerant amusement is pretty commendable.

But that of course was all nonsense. There was no real evidence that this mask had come from the grave of one of Agamemnon's followers; or indeed that Agamemnon had ever existed, or fought in the Trojan wars. That was the trouble with history, thought Lydia sadly, turning away from the case; it destroyed all one's pleasure in archaeology.

How much more pleasant to be one of the tourists now clustered obediently around the case under the direction of a wiry, middle-aged Greek lady with blue-tinted hair and a clear, carrying voice. "This is the death mask of one of the followers of Agamemnon, king of Mycenae," she was intoning with authority. "Agamemnon was murdered by his queen, Clytemnestra, and buried in the royal grave circle at Mycenae. All his followers were murdered at the same time. This gold mask, a portrait of the dead man, was fastened over the face of the corpse by means of a string tied at the back of the head. You can see the holes for the string in the edge of the mask." The group craned forward obediently. "The grave was excavated by the great German archaeologist, Schliemann, in 1876. Masks were also found in the other royal graves. Over here you will see the mask of Agamemnon himself . . ."

The little group moved on, their cameras dangling, their shuffling feet producing a deafening echo from the marble floor. How much more pleasure to be *sure!*

And yet, and yet—the tourists were missing so much in believing that this was one of the followers of Agamemnon. In the astonishment of that identification a far greater astonishment was swallowed up. How far more incredible it was that a mask so recognizable, so *modern* in expression, should have been devised more than three thousand years ago for the chieftain of a barbaric tribe—a tribe that covered the corruptible flesh of its dead heroes with incorruptible gold so that they might become gods.

The other, more famous mask—the one described as Agamemnon's—showed a face that was already that of a god; it was beautiful and terrifying, but quite inhuman. And there were other masks, faces with closed eyes and expressions of great suffering that expressed a horror and fear of death. The extraordinary thing about the first mask that Lydia had looked at was that it showed, quite simply, a man—a real, recognizable man who, if he spoke, would express thoughts and emotions that would be immediately understood today.

How subjective can you get? Lydia had thought crossly, skirting another conducted tour and peering into another case. Here there were two golden cups. Lions pursued each other energetically around the shallow bowl of the first, and on the second—an angular, heavy-looking goblet that gave an almost ecclesiastical impression—two little gold doves perched. In the next case was a great crown made out of delicate embossed gold; dozens of flat little gold disks, stamped with elaborate patterns, each one only an inch or so across; intricately carved seals and signet rings. And all of them—cups and crowns and disks and seals—were made of an intensely yellow gold, gold with no hint of red in it. And then, suddenly, she had come upon an astonishing ivory group of two women and a small boy—mother, daughter and grandson. The whole thing was only the size of an orange, but every flounce on the women's skirts was shown, every link of the daughter's necklace, every separate strand of her hair as it hung down her back. And they radiated affection and happiness—the mother with her arm protectively around her daughter's shoulders, the boy leaning across his grandmother's knee. Cups and swords and signet rings, crowns and ornaments, all made with a lightness of touch and a mastery of the technical problems involved that would still have been astonishing two thousand years later.

What sort of men were the people who made them? How did they live? What did they believe? There were no answers. Here, in half a dozen glass cases, was virtually all that was known about a civilization that must have been in its day as elaborate, as wealthy and as sophisticated as fifteenth-century Europe.

Now, remembering the bluff, smiling face from the Mycenaean grave, Lydia moved slowly up the long ramp, occasionally laying a hand reflectively against the enormous blocks of stone that enclosed the pathway. She emerged at last onto a vast, flat stone platform at the very top of the mound. There was a sudden impression of light and space and well-being after the menace of the great walls down below. The sunshine was dazzling, and a light wind blew steadily, shaking the little red poppies that grew everywhere in the cracks of the stones. On every side the plain stretched away, diced neatly into fields of orange trees. A mile to the south was the sea, with the fort floating in the bay and then the hills on the farther side, blue and rather misty.

The platform on which she was standing had been the floor of the palace. None of the buildings remained, but there were low walls about two feet high to show where the various rooms had been. At the top of the ramp was an enormous courtyard and then a throne room with a round open fireplace and the bases of four great pillars. There were mazelike suites of rooms which, the guidebook asserted confidently, had been the "women's quarters," and, finally, what had been a bathroom, its floor a single block of black stone grooved to let the water run away.

Nobody was in sight. Lydia sat down on one of the low walls and let the sun beat onto her closed eyes. Tiryns. The guidebook said that, in mythology, Tiryns had been the home of Hercules and Danaë. It was quite impossible to believe in Hercules on any level—so stupid and so unattractive. But Danaë, now, that was different. Not a little girl, as Mabuse had painted her, gazing up with innocent pleasure at the flickering golden motes that floated down toward her, but a terrified young woman imprisoned behind those great bronze-studded doors. Yes, she was real enough. But then again, Zeus, with his comic opera disguises—he wasn't credible here against the massive reality of those enormous walls. The gods of Tiryns must have been a harsher, crueler lot altogether—they would have had faces like the golden mask in Athens—austere, withdrawn and pitiless.

Gold again. Golden masks from the graves at Mycenae, Zeus wooing Danaë in a shower of gold at Tiryns—it's glitter and glamor seemed to surround these stony fortresses. Yellow gold.

Lydia opened her eyes and squinted in the sunlight. A few yards away from her feet the platform stopped and a wide area of grass and random slabs of rock stretched away to the western wall of the fortress. Against the green of the grass the quivering poppies were more vivid than ever. These were not the orange Flanders poppies, but a smaller and darker flower—exactly the color of blood. And that, too, was right for Tiryns. Yellow gold and blood.

Gold. But there had been nothing in the museum from Tiryns—all those masks and cups and swords had come from Mycenae. From Asiné some great earthenware pots, but from Tiryns nothing. There must have been treasures here, graves full of gold treasures . . .

Idly she scrambled down off the platform and started to pick her way through the slabs of rock; in the western wall, the guidebook said, was a hidden postern gate—a most interesting feature. Suddenly she stopped, badly startled. Right in front of her feet lay the body of a man, his face covered by a large straw hat. The trousers were faded and stained, the shirt crumpled and filthy—a workman's clothes. As she gasped, he sat up abruptly and looked at her. It was a long face, with blue eyes and a bony nose, and for a second Lydia had a sense of recognition. But then, confronted with his evident hostility, the impression faded.

"I'm so sorry," she started, and then, realizing that English would be no good, she brought out carefully her entire stock of modern Greek.

"Kal-ee-mer-a," she said politely.

"*Kalispera*," he replied promptly, and the trace of a smile appeared briefly on his face. Lydia was again disturbed by the sense of recognition. Then he spoke again, and at first, tensed and hoping to understand his Greek, Lydia heard the words only as a succession of whinnying noises. And then she blushed painfully.

What he had said, in a clear and aggressively cultured English voice, was, "And what a very pleasant evening it is, too. It's unusually warm for April this year," he went on unctuously. "It can sometimes be really quite chilly near the sea, even in May." He was really enjoying himself now. "It must be such a help to you to speak Greek. So few visitors do. I always think that if one makes no attempt to make contact with the natives, one *loses* so much in a foreign country. Don't you think so? Of course, not everyone is *able* . . ."

Lydia pulled herself together. She had remembered suddenly where she had seen him before, but for the moment that knowledge was better kept in reserve.

"Oh, yes, indeed," she said with equal smoothness, dropping the guidebook behind a rock and sitting down as gracefully as possible on the grass. "But there is of course an opposite danger. The English abroad are all too prone, I always think, just to go native. They abandon any attempt at keeping clean"—her eyes rested briefly on the filthy trousers—"and they make a great point of dissociating themselves at all costs from any other English travelers. But that is generally just an affectation, don't you think?"

There was an infinitesimal pause, and then, closing his eyes, he gave three dry little coughs. Then he opened his eyes again and smiled broadly. Lydia realized with relief and astonishment that he had been laughing.

"Oh, fair, very fair. Very pretty," he said appreciatively.

"Do you always bait innocent tourists who are only trying to be polite?" asked Lydia cautiously.

"No, no, I don't. I'm sorry. But it's been a bad day. I went to Mycenae and an American woman trod on my face. So I came here to be quieter and—you were the last straw. I beg your pardon," he added formally.

"That's all right. But mightn't it be more peaceful to sunbathe on something of a later date?"

"Sunbathe! Good heavens, I'm not sunbathing. I'm working. You see, well, this is actually all rather my sort of stuff. I'm . . ."

Lydia had her mouth open to say: *I know, I came to your lectures,* but there wasn't a moment.

"I'm a . . . a, well, a don, in fact." He managed to

make it sound apologetic. "At Oxford, you know. Now that . . ."

Good gracious, thought Lydia, fascinated, *he's going to tell me what "don" means.*

"During the term I teach the young and in the vacs—holidays, you know—I write books. And my period—the period I write books about—is what is called the Late Helladic period. Now, that is nothing more than the name that is given"—he was well away now—"to the Late Bronze Age in mainland Greece. It is also the Mycenaean period. It lasts, approximately . . ."

It was the voice of the professional teacher, the easy leisured periods of the man who knows that he can't be interrupted. *Swinging into the old routine*, thought Lydia. Blunt, his name was. Mondays and Wednesdays at ten.

". . . to about eleven hundred B.C. Now it is during this period that the Mycenaean civilization . . ."

He can't be more than thirty-five, thought Lydia with growing irritation, *despite the thinning hair*. And yet he was behaving like one of those old, old dons who believe that the world was created for them to instruct. *Is that what happens to all teachers?* she wondered suddenly. *Is that what's going to happen to me?*

". . . and by Mycenaean," he was saying kindly, "I mean not only Mycenae itself, but Tiryns and a place called Asiné too."

As long as I live, thought Lydia fervently, *may I please remember never to proffer information to total strangers.*

". . . a most elaborate civilization. A great many of their things—gold and silver ornaments and weapons and so on—have been found in graves at Mycenae. You can see them in Athens if you are interested. I myself have done a certain amount of digging—excavating, you know—over at Mycenae. In our first season . . ."

"Fascinating," said Lydia, getting briskly to her feet. Clearly nothing could stop him, but there was no reason why she should be made to listen all night.

He stood up and walked beside her, uninvited, as she turned back toward the platform. "Of course, great things may well emerge this summer."

"This summer?"

"Old Mrs. Adelmann is now dead."

Lydia stopped abruptly. "Adelmann?" It was the second time within a few hours that the name had been thrown at her.

"Dietrich Adelmann's widow."

"But who was he?"

"*Who?* the excavator of Tiryns." He spoke reverently. Every schoolboy knows. . . . How like an Oxford don to assume that one didn't know who or what Asiné was and yet to expect one to know all about some obscure German archaeologist.

"I thought Schliemann dug it and found nothing," she said unguardedly, watching a big green lizard scutter across a patch of stone and disappear behind one of the walls.

Fortunately he was too busy imparting information to be surprised that she had heard of Schliemann. "Yes, indeed. That is what is generally believed. And it may be so. What *is* certain is that he was so closely watched by the Greek authorities that he took nothing off the site. Nor did Dörpfeld, his assistant. But there was another young man, Dietrich Adelmann, a Bavarian. He was with Schliemann when he dug Tiryns in 1884, and he came back several years later on his own. For some reason the Greek authorities were less suspicious of him and he was left pretty much to his own devices."

"And did he find anything?"

"We're not sure. He wrote a letter to his wife during the dig which strongly suggests that he did. But then he died of fever within a fortnight."

"So anything he found is still in Greece?"

"That's it. But of course there mayn't have *been* anything." They had come to the edge of the platform now and stood looking out over the bay.

"What did Adelmann say to his wife in the letter?"

"He said: 'Soon, my beloved, I shall place on your brow a diadem more splendid than that of Troy and pour into your lap treasures beyong the dreams of all the seekers of gold.'"

"*What?*"

"Well, he was a German, you know. Flowery—"

"But just in a letter home?"

"Well, he admired Schliemann enormously, you see, and the whole emphasis of Schliemann's digging was on gold. He didn't care about history; he just wanted to dig up treasure. And he found it at Troy—extraordinary things, pots and rings and a couple of tremendous gold link diadems. He smuggled them all out of Turkey, and Sophia—Schliemann's wife, you know—was photographed wearing the diadem, and . . ."

He was talking now, Lydia noticed suddenly, not like a tired old don but like a young man with an enthusiasm. His eyes shone: his hands gesticulated.

"The Greek authorities of course didn't trust Schliemann an inch after that. Under Greek law, anything dug up belonged to the Greek government—as it does now— but they knew Schliemann would try to get it out of the country if he could. So when he was digging at Mycenae they sent a government official who watched every move and stopped him from getting anything out of the country. And the same thing happened when he came to dig Tiryns. Not that he found anything here."

"And nothing's been found at Tiryns since then?"

"No, it's all been dug very carefully, but apart from pottery and a few clay figures there wasn't a thing. So either Adelmann found the stuff, or else"—his voice was wistful—"it's still here to find. *Mind you*"—he had clearly remembered something—"it is a great mistake to attach disproportionate importance to gold and treasure. These grave finds, gold and so forth"—he glared at Lydia—"are interesting in themselves, of course, but pottery—just bits of ordinary pottery—are likely to be of far greater *historical* value. Being both intrinsically worthless and virtually indestructible they are found in enormous quantities on all these sites, and in many cases . . ."

The sun had dropped suddenly behind a bank of purple clouds above the hills on the far side of the bay. Separate golden rays, like the tinfoil halo on a Christmas angel, stretched up into a sky, turning from blue to apricot as Lydia watched. The bay was mottled purple and silver, every ripple edged with a gleam of light. On the plain below them the trees had lost their color and were round tufts of darkness, multiplied into infinity.

". . . you can date buildings and graves quite accurately from pottery, sometimes to within fifty or a hundred years. Schliemann, you see, treated what should be an exact science simply as a treasure hunt, and, except as a pioneer, you should not overrate the importance of his work."

He paused impressively. *And that's all until Wednesday*, thought Lydia. Aloud she said, "You know, I'm afraid I must go. I've got to get back to Nauplia." Her watch said half past five; it would take her at least half an hour to walk, and the wind was definitely chilly. "Thank you for telling me all this. It's been—" She wrestled with truth and came up with a compromise. "So very much of it was new to me."

"Oh. Well. I see. Good-bye, then. You have a car?" It was barely a question.

"Well, no. I shall walk—or hitch. I came by bus."

He paused for a moment. Then, "I've got a Vespa," he said at last. "If you wouldn't mind the back?"

"That would be marvelous."

But he went on looking at her, as though something remained to be settled.

"I—" he said. "My name is Blunt, Marius Blunt. How do you do."

Stanley and Livingstone, thought Lydia, shaking hands. *England forever. Those clothes are just a blind.*

THREE

At least he doesn't drive *like a don,* thought Lydia as Blunt put the scooter at the maze of railway lines at the entrance to the town without slackening speed.

"Where are you staying?" he shouted over his shoulder as the bucking subsided.

"Bourtzi."

A row of mimosa trees flashed past, luminous in the dusk, and they roared out onto the square and drew up in front of the Belle France. Lydia got off quickly, feeling suddenly ridiculous with her arms tightly around the waist of a man she hardly knew and didn't much like.

"Are you staying here?" she asked, mainly for something to say.

"No. Round the corner. King Otto."

"Oh. Well. Thank you so much."

"Not a bit. If you're here for a few days we might—" He hesitated. "Would you like to see Epidauros?"

"Well, actually, I'm here with someone else."

"Oh, I see." His interpretation of the remark was obvious.

"No, no," said Lydia without thinking. "An elderly lady."

"Oh. Oh, well."

"Thank you again," said Lydia. "Good-bye."

"Good-bye." He disappeared slowly into the dusk, pushing the Vespa, glancing back at her over his shoulder.

One of the waiters, whom Lydia recognized from lunchtime, came out of the hotel with a tray of coffee. When he saw Lydia he stopped and then hurried back into the hotel. A moment later a young man ran out, doing up his jacket as he ran, and stopped in front of her. He bowed formally, with a little click of the heels.

"Miss Barnett?"

"Yes?"

"My name is Callos. I am Mr. Nicos' cousin. I am sorry to tell you that Mr. Nicos has had an accident this afternoon."

He was young, perhaps twenty-five, with curly hair cut very short and a humorous face. He was neatly dressed in a well-pressed suit and highly polished shoes.

"He was knocked down by a motorcar and is now in the hospital. He has sent me to take his place." His English was almost faultless, and only his accent revealed him as Greek.

"But how terrible . . ." Lydia found it difficult to take in the significance of what he was saying—it sounded like a formula of some kind. "What—what happened?"

"He was knocked down," repeated Callos. "He is in no danger."

"I am so sorry—"

Lydia was at a loss in the face of this extreme correctness. "But isn't there anything we can do? Could we go to see him?"

"He is well looked after."

"Yes, I'm sure, but could we send him anything? Fruit, or—"

"No, nothing is necessary."

Now the waiter joined in reassuringly. "Not bad accident. This Callos very good driver. No need to be afraid."

The young man grinned suddenly, and Lydia found herself smiling too.

"No, of course not. I'm sure . . ."

He was a most surprising person to find driving a hired car, she reflected, but he was probably just helping his cousin out. All the same he was difficult to place. He reminded Lydia of the man who had asked Mrs. Erskine for matches at lunchtime—a younger version, of course, but he had the same manner: correct, formal—almost military.

"Well," she said lamely, "that's fine then. I'll tell Mrs. Erskine. I'm going back to the island now."

Callos was visibly startled. "You are *going* to the island now? But, where have you come from?"

"From Tiryns."

"You have been to Tiryns this afternoon?" He was making an extraordinary drama out of it all. "How did you go? You told Mr. Nicos you would not need the car until tomorrow."

"Oh, please don't worry about that. I changed my mind after I got to the island, and when I came back Mr. Nicos had disappeared and I didn't want to bother him. So I went by bus."

But he wasn't mollified. Lydia tried again. "I am a very keen sight-seer, and the guidebook said that Tiryns was only three kilometers away."

The guidebook. She glanced down at her hands. Handbag, dark glasses. No guidebook. Where then? And suddenly, clearly, she saw herself dropping the book into the grass behind a rock as she sat down to talk to Blunt. *Damn.* And all because of being clever. Mrs. Erskine's gleaming new guidebook sopping wet.

For a second she had forgotten Callos, but suddenly a solution occurred to her. And it would give him something to do—salve his pride.

"Mr. Callos, I'm sorry, but I've left Mrs. Erskine's guidebook at Tiryns and I've only just realized. If I leave it there all night it'll be ruined. If we take the car at once we could get there while there's still some light. Do you mind terribly?"

"You want to go back to Tiryns now? This evening?" He was suddenly very serious.

"Yes. Yes, please."

He hesitated for a moment. Then he said, "Very well. I will just . . . phone for the boat. To be waiting when you get back. Will you wait inside the hotel?" He took three steps and held the door authoritatively open. Lydia found herself following him. They were in a long open room scattered with tables. She stood awkwardly beside the door while Callos talked rapidly into a phone at the far end of the room, his hand shielding his mouth and the telephone receiver. The proprietor, standing behind his zinc-covered bar, and several of the dark, inscrutable men sitting at little tables watched her curiously under the glare of the fluorescent lights.

"Very well, I am ready." Callos opened the door for her again and then led the way toward the car.

He was, as the waiter had promised, a good driver, but he drove with such extreme caution that Lydia began to be afraid that the light would be gone altogether by the time they got there. "Could we go a bit faster?" she said, but Callos took no notice.

At Tiryns the attendant had gone, but the gate was closed only by a loose chain that they opened easily. It was very nearly dark, and the walls hung over them, the menace that they had only suggested during the day now almost palpable. Lydia was secretly relieved when Callos followed her into the ruins without being asked, but as they went up the ramp she became aware of the echo of their footsteps on the stones, and suddenly Callos' presence behind her was no longer reassuring. She could hear him breathing quickly, and all at once she was sure that the noise of their steps was covering up some other sound, one that she ought to hear.

She stopped, and Callos stopped behind her. In the silence she heard a car coming slowly down the track from the main road, out of sight behind the walls. Its engine roared once and was silent, and at that moment a ribbon of light appeared on the ground at her feet.

Lydia gasped.

"I am sorry to startle you." Callos' quiet voice was all urbanity. "I thought we needed a little light." He swung the flashlight upward, and the beam flickered high along the walls, picking out the enormous outline of the stones. "Shall we go on?"

Lydia's heart hit at her ribs as they started upward again. What, after all, did she know about Callos? He had appeared out of nowhere, claiming to be Nicos' cousin. He was only too clearly not the sort of young man who would normally be driving a car for foreign tourists. He must have other jobs, other motives . . . and she had got herself into this, she reflected bitterly. She had walked in with her eyes wide open.

The walls opened out suddenly and the darkness receded. There was still some light in the sky, and the stone of the platform glimmered under their feet.

"Over this way." Lydia almost ran across the platform and scrambled down into the grass. If she could just find the book and get out of this terrifying place and back to Nauplia. But Callos had moved equally fast, and the beam of his torch probed the darkness in front of her feet. The book was there; it was in her hand.

"Oh, what a relief. Now let's . . . let's go back." She

turned around to find Callos standing within a few inches. She tried to look at his face, but it was in darkness behind the beam of the flashlight.

"Allow me." Suddenly he took the book out of her hand.

"Oh . . . oh, thank you." She stepped around him and ran back across the platform and down onto the ramp, stumbling and gasping but never slackening speed. Callos followed, effortlessly, always just behind her, lighting the path with his flashlight. Even so, she almost fell several times and once twisted her foot on the uneven stones. Neither of them spoke again. When they reached the bottom, Lydia was gasping for breath, but Callos showed no sign of exertion.

As they climbed back into the Buick, Lydia could see the outline of the other car parked beside the track, about twenty yards away toward the main road. There were no lights.

Callos turned the car, and they bumped slowly up the track.

Who could it be in the other car? She didn't realize that she had spoken out loud until Callos said lightly, "Oh, young people . . . necking." But as their lights swept over the other car, Lydia saw two men sitting motionless side by side in the front seat.

Callos accelerated sharply as the car reached the main highway, and they roared back along the wide road toward Nauplia. Lydia felt suddenly unbearably tired. So much had happened in one day, ending with this ludicrous, upsetting incident. But what in fact had happened? Callos had turned on a flashlight unexpectedly and she had been startled. And yet, and yet . . . there had been a tension all the time, a sense of expectation, as if at any minute something—what?—might have happened. And it wasn't only herself, she was sure. Callos too had been expecting something. In fact, she realized suddenly, all the tension had come from him; what she had felt was his anxiety.

You're imagining the whole thing, she told herself crossly as they drove into the town and the streetlights shone on a laughing group outside the door of a café. *You can't even be alone with a man at night without expecting him to assault you.* But that wasn't right either.

It was rather, she realized suddenly, that Callos had been expecting *her* to assault *him.* But—

They were back at the Belle France now. There was no sign of a boat beside the quay, and Callos, with a mutter of "Telephone," disappeared immediately into the hotel.

"Lydia!" A glad cry. Henry James was bouncing up and down like a puppy—a puppy who hadn't seen her for weeks and whose whole day was being made by her arrival. *"Hello!* Come and have a drink!" He made sweeping come-on-over gestures. "How lovely to *see* you again!"

"Hello," said Lydia uncertainly. Their friendship had evidently blossomed while she was away.

"Come and meet Booby!"

Booby had somehow missed the excitement. He was sitting quietly at the table with his pudgy hands clasped loosely in his lap and a sweet, enormous smile all over his moon-shaped face. He was small and plump, and tufts of fluffy gray hair surrounded the dome of the eggiest egghead Lydia had ever seen.

"How do you do?" He hung his huge head sideways and smiled at her shyly.

"Mr. Benedict, Miss Barnett."

"It is spelled B-U-B-I," he said confidingly, "and was not originally intended as a description of my appearance." The smile was infinitely charming. "My parents were great Anglophiles, and they christened me Robert." *French?* wondered Lydia. Those rolling r's under the American twang. . . . "But my schoolfellows could get no nearer than Booby. And so, you see . . ." Farther east than Paris, she decided. Austria? Armenia, even? She smiled back at him.

"Have you been sight-seeing?" Henry was still bouncing slightly. "Where did you go?"

"I went to Tiryns, and then left my guidebook behind and had to go back." She laughed apologetically. "Did . . . did the *Arcady* come in finally?"

Henry pointed across the square, and Lydia saw at the very end of the quay three white masts and a cluster of lights.

Bubi gave a gentle sigh. "And now I am waiting for cameramen from Athens. And it is so important that we do not lose more time."

"I liked your Mrs. Eskin, was it?" Henry broke in.

"Erskine. Yes, she's a dear."

"Is she a relation?"

"No, an employer."

"*Employer?*"

Lydia was suddenly aware of Callos standing just behind her chair. "The boat is here, Miss Barnett."

"Oh, well, I must go then."

"But, Lydia, you'll have a drink with us?"

"No, really, Henry, it's after seven. Good-bye. Good-bye, Mr. Benedict."

"Good-bye, Miss Barnett. And my name is Bubi. I am Bubi for everyone."

FOUR

The silence woke Lydia. For a long time she struggled with the idea: *What has happened? What is wrong?* and then with a wrench she lifted herself up out of sleep and into consciousness. A narrow shaft of sunlight streamed into the room and fell across the end of her bed. The sibilant movement of the sea on the rocks below her window served only to emphasize the silence around her—a silence that, even as she stretched and turned over, was broken for a moment by the sound of a girl's voice somewhere outside and an answering laugh. Lydia smiled to herself and stretched again with an enormous sense of well-being.

The previous night she had been so tired that she had hardly glanced at the hotel or at her room and had fallen into bed immediately after dinner. Now she got out of her bed to explore. The room was bare and white, with a low, vaulted ceiling and one narrow window. The walls and ceiling were marked with irregular pits, like the footprints of some huge animal in the snow. The floor was tiled, and the whole effect was one of cleanliness and space. Outside her window a tiny, curved balcony gave a miraculous view of Nauplia in deep purple shadow, hidden from the morning sun by the great jut of rock above the town. The sea below her was like a plate, flat and shiny, and a shoal of brown fishes nosed eagerly at the rocks below the fort. A moment later she saw why. From somewhere just underneath her window a brown paper parcel flew through the air and burst as it hit the surface of the water. Dozens of chickens' feet, tied together in pairs and looking like pale underwater animals, drifted and wavered down to the seabed while the brown paper floated slowly away along the surface. The shoal of fish, which had exploded like a rocket when the parcel hit the water, darted back in twos and threes and started to peck at the claws.

Chicken for lunch, thought Lydia. She went to have a shower.

"Now is the time," she sang loudly under the rush of hot water, "when we must say good-bye." Happiness and excitement splashed around in the shower with her. By the end of yesterday, she realized, she had been feeling so tired that things had seemed gloomy and menacing. But now here was Greece and sunshine and the wine-dark sea full of chickens' feet just outside her window and the whole holiday still in front of her.

It was no moment for half measures or old clothes. Mrs. Erskine's generous salary had been spent before it was earned, and she considered herself with satisfaction in the mirror over the dressing table. *And who are you out to impress?* she asked herself sarcastically. *Mrs. Erskine?* But her pleasure was undiminished. Henry James then? No, really . . . and as for that boring don, she'd have to wear a Mycenaean death mask before he'd notice anything about her appearance at all. Smiling at the thought, she went off to look for breakfast.

Lydia had half expected carpets and hall porters, a smart tourist hotel. But everything here was as white and bare and silent as her room had been. There was a high gray tower and a wide courtyard with a great plump cascade of purple flowers spilling down from the roof, and everywhere between the gray stone fortifications and through the windows, there were dazzling glimpses of the sea. There was no one in sight, and it was very quiet.

She found Mrs. Erskine on a terrace looking over toward Nauplia. She was gesturing energetically at one of the little girls in black.

"She's a honey," said Mrs. Erskine, "but she really doesn't understand English." With generous gestures she poured water from an imaginary kettle into an imaginary teapot. The girl giggled but didn't move.

"Perhaps this is the moment for my phrase book," said Lydia. She went back to her room and got the small brown pamphlet she had bought in London.

"Tsigh-ee?" she read out doubtfully. The girl at once nodded and disappeared into the hotel. A wave of giggles washed back behind her.

"It's like a fairy story," said Lydia. "A magic castle, all quite silent, with silent, magic servants."

"Well, I shall need something stronger than magic tea, I can tell you, to put me back on my feet after all that lighter fluid we drank yesterday. But you're marvelous with that book. Does it have 'Bring me some toast and marmalade'? That'll be the next problem."

"Well, it's got 'In the afternoon I would like to hire a bicycle.' How about that?"

"Good gracious, let me look. . . . Oh, there are some fascinating things here. 'I cannot move my *blank*.' What a remarkable thing to put in a book. Well, well."

She glanced apologetically at Lydia, and as they both started to laugh there was a warning rattle of china and three little girls appeared, carrying among them a heavy tray with a teapot and cups and saucers.

"They're so *cute*," said Mrs. Erskine, gazing at them. "I keep feeling the biggest one ought to unscrew in the middle and you could fit the other two inside. You know those wooden dolls?"

"I hadn't thought of that. To me, girls in uniform are just the upper fourth or lower fifth according to size. It's a job that marks you. . . . Milk or lemon?"

"Oh, lemon, I think, please. Well, if you want to know" —Mrs. Erskine settled herself comfortably—"it seems to me that you've been less marked by it than I would have expected. You're not prissy, you know what I—"

"Mrs. Erskine?"

Lydia looked around. There had been no sound, but suddenly they were there—two men in military uniform with highly polished leather belts and boots, standing stiffly at attention.

"I am Mrs. Erskine." She was clearly disconcerted.

One of the men stepped forward and bowed briefly.

"Major Papandros, Nauplia police." It was the man who had tried to borrow matches on the terrace at the Belle France yesterday. And suddenly everything about his formal manner and upright bearing was explained. But in contrast to the day before, his expression was grim and the black eyes glittered.

"May I ask if you have been in touch with Mr. Callos this morning?"

"In touch?"

"Have you spoken to him on the telephone? Or seen him?"

"No. No, I've never seen him."

"I saw him," Lydia said. "Yesterday evening. About seven o'clock. He drove me out to Tiryns and back."

"Yes. Yes, I know." Major Papandros dismissed her intervention and turned again to Mrs. Erskine. "But you have not seen him this morning? Or spoken to him?"

"No. But . . ."

"I see. Well, I must ask you both—" He stopped for a moment and looked hard at Mrs. Erskine. "No, for the moment it will be enough if Miss Barnett comes with me."

"Comes with you?" said Lydia.

"Your car has been stolen."

"But—"

"I should like to ask you a few questions."

"If you need to ask questions, Major Papandros, I suggest you talk to me." Mrs. Erskine's voice was suddenly firm—and ice cold with displeasure. "I hired that car. I employed Mr. Nicos. What is it you want to know?"

Papandros adjusted quickly. "Madame, forgive me. I am anxious only to save you inconvenience. I should like Miss Barnett to come with me to my office now to answer a few routine questions about the car—when you last saw it, where it was—that sort of thing."

"I will come, too."

"Madame, that will not be necessary." His tone was perfectly correct—but the authority was clear.

Lydia interposed quickly. "I don't mind going."

Mrs. Erskine hesitated and then said with great emphasis, "If Miss Barnett is treated with even the slightest degree of disrespect, Major Papandros, I shall telephone at once to the United States ambassador . . . and to the British ambassador."

Papandros bowed. There was a pause.

"I'll just get my bag, then."

As she went into the hotel Lydia heard Major Papandros say politely to Mrs. Erskine, "Have no anxiety, Madame."

The boat at the jetty was not the usual one belonging to the hotel but a powerful launch with a crest on the side. Major Papandros hurried Lydia on board. The other officer remained on the quay and saluted as they pulled away in a flurry of spray. Conversation was impossible against the roar of the engines, and Lydia sat awkwardly in silence watching Papandros' abstracted face. As he stepped ashore, an officer who had been waiting on the quay sprang forward, saluted and started to talk urgently to him, gesturing emphatically. Papandros frowned, nodded twice and turned briskly toward an official-looking car that was waiting with its engine running. Then, suddenly remembering Lydia, he hesitated and turned back.

"Miss Barnett, there has been an unexpected development, and I shall not, after all, be able to take the time this morning to ask you . . ." He paused as a new idea struck him. "No, after all," he said, "it will be good if you will accompany me, as you will be able to . . ." His voice trailed away, and he gestured with sudden uncharacteristic vagueness. Then, without waiting for a reply, he motioned her into the back of the car, signaled to the driver and sprang in after her. The car moved off swiftly across the square.

Outside the town the driver took a turn to the right, away from the road to Athens, and the car shot forward as he slammed down the accelerator. The road twisted among hills for a couple of miles and then ran out into a wide, flat valley with fields and orange trees on either side. There was a distant view of mountains.

Lydia glanced at Papandros. He was frowning deeply and staring straight out at the road ahead of them.

"Major Papandros, please tell me what has happened. Has Mr. Callos . . ."

He turned slowly and looked directly into her face.

"I do not know where Callos is," he said carefully. "I am anxious to find out."

"But—"

"Your car—the car you hired—had disappeared this morning."

"Yes, you told Mrs. Erskine. But you surely can't think that Mr. Callos . . ."

Major Papandros continued to look at her, and his expression, she realized with surprise, was now one of real dislike, almost of distaste. Then, without saying anything more, he turned away to look at a small white village that was being snatched past their windows.

"Major Papandros," Lydia tried again. "I really don't understand. How do you *know* that the car had been stolen? We have heard nothing. If you don't know where Mr. Callos is, could he not just have driven off somewhere . . ." Her voice died away. Major Papandros had not moved, and it was suddenly clear to her that he had already said all, for the moment, that he was prepared to say.

Just then the car slackened speed, turned sharply to the left and started to jolt along a rough track beside a steep hillside of grass and rocks. A flat, sandy beach opened out ahead of them, stretching away for nearly a mile. The car stopped abruptly, and Papandros got out and walked quickly across the sand toward a little group of men and vehicles at the edge of the sea. Lydia followed more slowly.

The beach was in shadow here, cold and rather forbidding with the hill looming above it. A long wooden jetty had been built out into the sea for perhaps fifty yards; its timbers were gray and there were a few planks missing, but it was still serviceable. The men were standing just at the point where the jetty reached the sand. There were three men in uniform, two khaki-painted cars and a small truck. The truck had been backed down to the very edge of the sea and was standing with its back wheels in three or four inches of water. As Major Papandros appeared, the uniformed figures saluted smartly and they all turned to look out toward the sea. When Lydia got nearer she could see what they were looking at. A long, shallow curve of gray metal was just visible above the surface of the water a few yards out from the end of the jetty. In the same moment she realized what it was.

"Major Papandros . . ."

"Yes, Miss Barnett. Your car has been found," he said in a curious, expressionless voice, and he turned to look at her.

At that moment a hunched, gleaming figure heaved itself out of the water a few yards from the shore, and for a moment Lydia hardly recognized it as human. The man's body, arms and legs were covered by a black rubber suit, and he was carrying two metal cylinders on his back. As he waded in toward the shore he took off the glass mask which had covered his face, and Lydia saw him shrug and say something to Papandros. A moment later Papandros gave a command, a winch mounted on the back of the truck started to turn, and a steel rope that had been lying slack on the sand sprang into life, snaking steadily into the truck, lifting itself gradually from the water until it stretched, taut and trembling, from the winch to a point about fifty yards out from the shore, pointing like an arrow straight at the long flat curve of gray metal. Suddenly the winch started to whine and the rope stopped moving. Then slowly, hesitatingly, it started to inch itself onto the drum again. Papandros nodded.

For the next twenty minutes they simply stood and waited, with the roar of the winch all around them. It was turning painfully, a few inches at a time, and Lydia found that her eyes came back to it again and again. Without that reassurance it would have been impossible to tell that the gray shape out in the sea was moving at all. Once she asked Papandros, "But how could the car have got out there? What do you think has happened?" and he answered in a voice of polite irony, "Miss Barnett, if you take a powerful American car, wedge its throttle open and put it on that"—he nodded at the jetty—"it is likely to fall off the end." After that she didn't speak again.

Gradually the curve of the metal grew higher and higher above the water, and at last the back window was visible, and then the handle of the trunk. The winch started to turn more rapidly. The whole group of watchers moved down to the very edge of the water, intent on the big car that was now clearly visible above the shallow water, moving steadily nearer and nearer. And then they were all in the water up to their knees, pressing forward to touch the car and to peer in through its closed windows.

Lydia hardly knew what she had expected—certainly not that the sea could have caused such havoc in so short a time. All the upholstery was in tatters, and the metal framework of the seats was almost bare. Soaking and messy, the leather padding lay on the floor or was twined in the metal springs or draped on the steering wheel— just as the water, pouring out now through the floor and the cracks around the doors, had left it. Lydia stared, appalled and unbelieving.

Major Papandros gave a little grunt, as though he had

expected such a sight, and then waded back to the shore. The winch turned for another few moments, rapidly now, until the car was standing immediately behind the truck. Then it stopped abruptly, and the silence seemed to bring with it—indecision. Major Papandros, Lydia, the driver and the three anonymous uniformed figures stood and just looked at the car.

Suddenly Papandros shook himself and nodded to the soldier who had been working the winch. Taking an iron bar out of the truck, the man went to the back of the gray car and with one rapid movement broke open the lock of the trunk. The lid swung up.

There was a moment of silence, and then Papandros stepped forward, reached into the trunk and turned the body over onto its back.

His clothes were soaked, and the seawater had flattened the short dark hair against his scalp, but Callos hadn't died by drowning.

As though holding other thoughts at bay, Lydia's mind repeated over and over again: *So that was why . . . that was why . . . that was why. . . .* That was why they had used golden masks. The face of a man done violently to death is too terrible to look at. Gold was a protection for the living.

Suddenly she was aware of a great stir of activity around her—as though the whole group of men had been under a spell, sleepwalking, from the moment when the winch began to turn, and now the spell had been broken. Papandros was talking, giving orders, shouting in a voice unnecessarily loud; two of the soldiers were lifting the body out onto the ground; another had started one of the cars and had roared away up the beach toward the track in a splatter of sand; and now Papandros had caught her elbow in a grip so fierce that she tried to cry out from her gritty throat, and he was hurrying her up to the beach and thrusting her rapidly into his car; the driver was backing and turning, flinging them from side to side; and then once again they were out on the road with the white villages whipping past the windows, heading back toward Nauplia.

In his office Papandros said grimly, "*Now,* Miss Barnett, you will answer my questions."

He pressed a buzzer on his desk, and a young soldier entered the room quietly and slid into a seat by the door. Strips of sunlight filtered into the room through the closed shutters, but Papandros' face was in shadow.

"Your full name, please."

"Lydia Anne Barnett." The young soldier's pencil whispered across his pad.

"Age?"

"Twenty-seven."

Papandros himself wrote nothing down but checked her answers against a piece of paper on his desk.

"You are traveling as companion to Mrs. Erskine?"

"Well—" *Oh, let it go.* "Yes."

"Where were you born? . . . and educated? . . . you entered Greece? . . . and stayed. . ." The routine questions followed one after another. Suddenly, without warning, Papandros started to shout.

"Where did you go yesterday afternoon?"

Lydia jumped. "Yesterday?"

"Where did you go?"

"To—to Tiryns."

"And whom did you go to meet?"

"To meet? No one."

Papandros leaped to his feet, strode around the desk and stood over her, beating his fist on the desk, roaring at her. *"Who? Who? Tell me who!"* His eyes glittered, and he was clearly longing to hit her.

"No one, honestly. *No one."*

Papandros was silent, and after a moment he turned and went back to his chair. Lydia's heart was thudding, but as the wave of fear receded, she started suddenly to feel angry.

"Major Papandros, this is perfectly ridiculous," she said, stuttering slightly. "You are treating me as—as if I were—were *guilty* of something. An appalling thing has happened, but it's no good bullying me. It would be more to the point surely to find out about Mr. Callos' movements yesterday."

"You'll have to do better than that, Miss Barnett," he said tiredly. "Lieutenant Callos' movements yesterday are known to me."

"Lieutenant?"

Papandros watched her expressionlessly, his anger gone.

"That can hardly come as a surprise to you, Miss Barnett. But let us get back to the point." He leaned forward across the desk. "Listen. You arrived in Nauplia at midday yesterday. You pretended to go out to the island but returned immediately and disappeared for more than two hours. I want to know who you saw."

"But this is nonsense. I went to look at Tiryns."

"If you went to Tiryns, as you claim, why did you not go in your car?"

"When I got back from the island, Mr. Nicos had disappeared and I didn't want to disturb him, so I took a bus."

"It won't do, Miss Barnett," said Papandros wearily. "You told Mr. Nicos that you would not need the car till the next day. But you returned within ten minutes. Whom did you meet yesterday afternoon?"

"Are you," started Lydia slowly after a pause. "Do you think that I was . . . in some way connected with Mr. Callos' death?"

"I know that *personally* you were not"—he leaned heavily on the word—"because you did not leave the island between seven o'clock last night and nine thirty this morning. But that in itself tells me nothing. I still wish to know"—and he tapped his pencil on the desk, one tap for each word—"who—you—went—to—meet—yesterday—afternoon."

Lydia looked at him for several moments without speaking. At last she said, in a carefully controlled voice, "Look. Please let me get this straight once and for all. I went to Tiryns yesterday afternoon to—to *look* at it. As a tourist. I went by myself. The only people I spoke to the entire time were the bus driver and an English don—teacher that I met there."

"An English don?" Papandros was suddenly interested.

"An Englishman who teaches at Oxford University."

"Do you know his name?"

"Marius Blunt."

"You saw Mr. Blunt at Tiryns?"

"Yes."

Papandros made a sign, and the young soldier got up and left the room.

Lydia felt a prickle of hope. Papandros clearly knew about Blunt, and Blunt would at least confirm her story.

For a few minutes they sat in silence, and then the telephone on the desk rang. Papandros hesitated and went out of the room. Lydia could hear him speaking in the outer office. Two or three minutes later he came back and said slowly, "Very well, Miss Barnett. I shall not need you anymore for the moment. You may go."

She almost ran down the wide marble stairs, and as she reached the hall a tall figure came rapidly in out of the sunlight to meet her.

"Oh, Mr. Blunt! Thank goodness you're here—it's been so awful—I—I can't tell you—" Words tumbled over each other. "The most awful things have happened—I—"

"Miss Barnett." His tone stopped her dead. She found that she had put out her hand to him as she ran forward, and now she stood still, foolishly, her arm still outstretched.

"Excuse me." Carefully he stepped around her and went up the stairs two at a time.

She was in a narrow street now with little shops on either side. The shops were closed and silent, and the windows of the tall houses above them were shuttered. There was no one about, and there was no noise except the sound of her footsteps, hollow and echoing. She was alone, quite alone.

The street opened into a long narrow square with high pink houses on either side. It, too, was deserted, and the dazzling sun filled it like a tank. In the middle of the square was a single iron bench. Lydia sat down and dropped her head into her hands. She found that she was trembling uncontrollably. Slowly, something incongruous and horrible forced itself on her attention: her shoes, the blue shoes that had been new that morning, were now, suddenly, all wrinkled, and stained with crusted white blotches. Appalled, she stared at them, and at that moment a shadow fell across the gravel beside her feet.

"Lydia?" It was Henry James. "Lydia, whatever's the matter?" His voice was warm, affectionate, concerned.

"Henry? Oh, Henry, I've got my *shoes* wet." Stormily she burst into tears.

"Oh, good gracious. What? I say. Don't do that."

Briskly he sat down beside her, producing a large handkerchief and laying a heavy arm along her shoulders.

"This won't do, you know. You know that? Can't have this. My goodness."

Solicitously he clucked and patted, exclaimed and clucked and patted.

After a while he said, "I'll bet you haven't had any lunch."

"No." Lydia blew her nose. "No, I haven't. But I've got to go and—"

"No. Food first."

"Henry, I'm so ashamed."

"Oh, nonsense."

Lydia looked at her watch. It was nearly two o'clock.

"I don't know what you've got to do," said Henry, "but you won't be able to do it for another hour at least. Everything shuts for lunch."

"Those shops . . . and the houses?" Sanity peered through.

"Shops, and the post office, and the boat out to the hotel. Everything. Now you just do as I say."

Weakly, gratefully, she nodded, and Henry shepherded her quickly across the square and into another silent street.

"Not the Belle France, I think, don't you?" It was as though the word TACT had come on in colored lights. Even while feeling grateful—and she realized suddenly what her face must be looking like—Lydia grinned. There was an elephantine quality about the workings of Henry's mind, and at the same time a transparency. Can one be both elephantine *and* transparent? she wondered, cheering up. But there was no doubt that Henry was.

A few yards farther, and they plunged through a swinging bead curtain into impenetrable blackness laced with smoke.

"Okay, darling," said Henry briskly, "let's budge up then." He was already holding her hand far too tightly, ostensibly to guide her between the crowded tables, and now he inserted her into what seemed to be a wooden booth with high-backed seats.

"So, honey bun, what's new?" A different Henry, this. But then blondness gleamed through, and Lydia saw with relief that they were sharing a table with Mary-Lou.

"Where's your friend?"

"Location." A taciturn girl, Mary-Lou.

"Annie gone too?"

"Guess so."

"Good. Now, Lydia"—he leaned across the table—"what would you like?"

In the end, of course, it was olives and sardines and tomatoes followed by broiled fish and green salad and retsina.

"It's what they do best," conceded Henry.

"It's *all* they do," said Mary-Lou scornfully, drinking black coffee.

Anyway, it tasted like heaven, and Lydia concentrated silently for a long time. Peace reigned.

"Trouble," said Henry suddenly, as a tall woman with faded hair pulled sharply back from a bumpy forehead marched into the restaurant and came toward their table.

"Bubi wants you," she said to Henry without preliminaries. Her voice was sharp and nasal, American, but quite different from either Mrs. Erskine's roller-coaster vowels or Mary-Lou's all-day drawl. She was wearing a buttoned seersucker housedress and lace-up shoes that had formerly been white. Bony hands hung by her sides.

"Hell!" Henry shoveled in another forkload of fish. "But, Annie," he said indistinctly, "I've only just started lunch."

"Come on," Annie said flatly. Henry stood up meekly and clambered out of the booth.

"Lydia, dinner? Do say yes." He took some notes from his wallet and tucked them under the plate. "We haven't talked at all yet."

"Well, Henry, no, I don't really think . . . But thank you all the same."

"Well, we'll be in touch later. I'm terribly sorry about this—okay, okay, Annie, I'm with you." And they were gone.

Lydia returned to her fish.

Mary-Lou, it appeared, had no plans for leaving, and she stayed just where she was. She was all in white today —white silk jersey and white silk trousers. Companionable but undemanding, scornful as a Persian kitten, she sat and watched Lydia eat.

Wonderful stuff, food, thought Lydia. Instant energy. The soul's barometer rising. This term's Special Prize for Constructive Kindness goes to H. James, Lower III. Hooray! And the wooden spoon to H. Papandros for absolutely everything. How *defiant* one feels, fed! *Under the bludgeonings of chance*—now there was a poem that could only have been written after lunch—*my head is bloody, but unbowed*. And talking about bloody—that *Blunt*. What in heaven's name did he think he was up to? Treating her like yesterday's cold potatoes, walking around her like a cat's mess on the stair carpet . . .

"You oughta put that blue in your hair too."

Lydia was taken entirely off-guard; Mary-Lou had volunteered a remark.

"Oh. Yes. Well, perhaps. Actually I'm not mad on ribbon in the hair."

But Mary-Lou hadn't been trying to start an argument. Silence renewed itself. Lydia ate on.

But toward the end of the fish her social conscience began to nag. "Which part of the States do you come from?" she asked, feeling that the conversational onus was now on her.

"Mazura."

"Oh, yes." *Try to sound as if it means something.*

"Arlington, Mazura."

"Oh." *Oh, dear.* "Is this your first—er—movie?"

The effect was astonishing.

"Movie!" Mary-Lou's face snapped into life. "This ain't a *movie*. That lousy one-shot. All he ever shoots is islands. *Islands!* He said I had a real movie face and he'd give me a real part—lines and everything—and a hundred dollars for every day on set. I was supposed to have a private yacht, special costumes, my own dresser—dresser!" She laughed with elaborate irony. "You saw that Annie? All she's ever done for me since I got here is to tell me to shut my face if I try to talk to him."

Lydia gazed. It was like seeing a slot machine in the act of spilling the jackpot.

"Bastard. Private yacht! I'd like to—I'd like to—" She smoldered.

But they shall be the terrors of the earth, muttered Lydia to herself. *Good heavens.* "But"—she was groping —"is this Henry?"

"Henry?"—scornfully. "No, Bubi. And *now*"—she got back into gear—"he says he's going home, do the rest back there. And I'm in this dump a whole month. I might just as well never have come."

"Oh, dear, I'm so sorry." It was totally inadequate, but there didn't seem to be anything more constructive to say. "You don't like Nauplia?"

"No."

"Well, I do hope—" She floundered. "That—that things go better and—er—so on. Is there anything I could do?"

But Mary-Lou had run out of gas again. Lydia waited a few minutes, feeling uncomfortable, and then, guiltily remembering Mrs. Erskine, she clambered to her feet.

"Look, I'm terribly sorry, but I'm afraid I ought to . . . I really must go. Good-bye. See you—see you around."

Lydia went, feeling ashamed. She had been totally unhelpful, and poor Mary-Lou clearly *had* something of a grievance against Bubi. Probably his motives hadn't been so purely cinematic, but she hadn't said anything about that. . . . And so Mary-Lou wanted to be a film star. It seemed such an odd ambition. Money, of course, and fame —yes, and those, of course, would bring love and happiness. *Just what we all want when you really get down to it,* thought Lydia resignedly, threading her way through the narrow streets.

A cluster of little tourist shops with postcards and pots and piles of multicolored dresses outside, and then she turned the corner by the Belle France and ran slap into a busy scene.

Mrs. Erskine was sitting on a suitcase in the full glare of the sun, weeping with great energy. Beside her on the gravel was a pile of luggage among which Lydia recognized her own blue suitcase. The manager of the Belle France and the young policeman who had stayed out at the Bourtzi with Mrs. Erskine that morning were both talking at once, partly to Mrs. Erskine, partly to each other. Two waiters and four of the inscrutable, black-suited gentlemen who were always to be seen on the Belle France terrace were watching with the cautious interest one accords a dog fight.

"No, I won't," sobbed Mrs. Erskine loudly. "I won't stay another night in this horrible place. I'm going to go right back to Athens. Tonight. And you just get me a car." She swung around toward the manager and saw Lydia. "Oh, *honey!*"

Lydia found that she was standing with her arms around Mrs. Erskine and that Mrs. Erskine was sobbing more loudly than ever. "Isn't it awful? Isn't it *awful?*"

The black-suited gentlemen stirred and moved a step closer.

"Miss Barnett," said the young officer, exasperation in his voice, "I am trying to tell Mrs. Erskine that Major Papandros does not wish you and Mrs. Erskine to leave Nauplia until our inquiries have progressed further."

"I have two very nice rooms," the manager of the Belle France said quickly.

"We'll have to stay, you know," said Lydia as gently as she could. "You don't want to go back to the Bourtzi?"

"No, they were stealing our things—"

"*Stealing?*"

"Yes, going through our suitcases."

The black-suited gentlemen where so close now that Lydia could see the individual gleam of interest in each dark eye.

"Not now." She looked around hectically. "Let's . . . why not take the rooms here?"

Mrs. Erskine stopped crying. "You really reckon we've got to stay if the guy says so?"

"I'm afraid so."

"Okay." It was only a whisper.

The group dispersed abruptly. The manager and the waiters picked up the suitcases and disappeared into the hotel, Mrs. Erskine and Lydia followed, and the black-suited gentlemen drifted sadly away.

In the doorway of the hotel Lydia came face to face with Marius Blunt. He blushed a dark red and his mouth opened, but he didn't move out of the way. Lydia and Mrs. Erskine stopped. Still he didn't move. With her full strength Lydia pushed viciously at his chest, and he fell back sharply with a loud, bony cracking sound against the side of the door. Then she grasped Mrs. Erskine by the elbow and guided her into the hotel.

"Why, Lydia!" said Mrs. Erskine, peering over her shoulder with interest as they started up the stairs. "Whoever was that? Do you know him?"

"I will tell all," said Lydia grimly. She felt more cheerful than she had for hours.

FIVE

Héllènes nous étions . . . et sommes avec vous.

This was yet another Greece—not the gold and blood of the Mycenaeans, not the cool perfections of classical Athens, not even the world of hot showers and tourist buses. This was the Romantic Age.

TO THE HEROIC DEFENDERS OF THE NATION
TO THE MEMORY OF THE PHILHELLENES
WHO DIED FOR
INDEPENDENCE
GREECE, THE KING, AND THEIR GRATEFUL
COMPANIONS IN ARMS

And then the long list of names, arranged tidily battle by battle. Most of them were German or French—Schilder, Diedrichs, Boneparte (*Paul, fils de Lucien, Prince de Ganino*), but a few were English. How ignorant one is, thought Lydia. One knows about Byron (there he was, Number 10 under *Missolonghi*), but what about Higginson and Fitzgibbon, who died at Poros? or *Murray* (*Lord*) *Charles, fils du duc d'Atholl*, who was killed at Castoun? Byron had somehow been established as *the* Englishman who died for Greek freedom, but here were all these others who had done no less.

The memorial was infinitely touching—and partly perhaps because it was so badly painted. In white lettering on a black background it was acknowledged with pride as the handiwork of: *Monsieur A. H. Touret, Lieutenant Colonel, Chevalier de plusieurs ordres. Le 8/20 mai 1841.*

Who was he? wondered Lydia. Was he a Frenchman who had fought for Greek independence and stayed on to enjoy it? Why else, twenty years later, should he have been chosen to paint the memorial?

For this wasn't just any town. Nauplia had been the capital for nearly ten years after Greece became independent, which was why perhaps, she thought, it was still so definitely a town—almost, still, a city—when in terms of size alone it was little more than an overgrown village.

Lydia had found the memorial quite by accident. It had taken the whole afternoon to restore Mrs. Erskine's morale, but by five o'clock, when they had discussed everything three times over and arrived at no explanation, Mrs. Erskine was quite ready to go down and have tea outside and "see if there are any nice people." And Lydia had reflected with gratitude that the move to the Belle France might yet turn out to be a blessing. Their rooms were nice, as the manager had promised, with a wooden balcony connecting them. From it, as Lydia pointed out to Mrs. Erskine, they would be able to lean over and spit on the heads of the dark, inscrutable gentlemen drinking their coffee. But for all that, Lydia felt privately, it was a bit of a comedown after the bare whiteness and silence of the Bourtzi.

She had left Mrs. Erskine discussing Iowa with an American lady off one of the tourist buses and set out by herself to explore the town. She had not expected such charm—or such wit. The houses were square and solid, with large sash windows and slatted wooden shutters and sometimes a carved stone doorway or a pediment, but there formality ended. There were pink houses and white houses and every conceivable shade of yellow and ocher; and even blue houses of exactly the same tired, dusty color that Lydia had seen on the beehives above Corinth and then again on the fishing boats in the harbor—the color of the sea with the shine taken out. Many of them were shabby and run-down, their plaster chipped and their shutters gray and unpainted, but the colors still made them look gay and lighthearted—theatrical, almost. And this effect was heightened by the way in which the town hung on the side of its hill: many of the streets were no more than wide stone stairways, opening up improbable vistas over pink curly-tiled roofs and domes and over delicate iron balconies sprouting at random from the colored houses, each one stuffed full and spilling over with carnations and roses and geraniums. It was all enchanting.

Lydia had felt soothed and happy. With her sunglasses and her guidebook she had felt herself again an innocent and law-abiding tourist, no longer a suspect who had been interrogated by the police. She wandered about for nearly an hour, lost but unworried. And then, just as she was beginning to wonder where she was, she had come to the solid gray stairway with its domed gateway and iron grille. Beyond that was a narrow whitewashed terrace, from which she could look down through the branches of orange trees to the roofs of the town and to the bay and the fort and the farther shore. The terrace too was bursting with flowers; white irises grew in a wide bed along the edge, white phlox and tobacco flowers bulged out of flower beds made from white-painted gasoline cans, and there were vines twisting up the gray wall of the church at the back of the terrace. Lydia had sat down on a bench against the church wall, and had started to think.

In talking to Mrs. Erskine, she had leaned heavily on such elements of optimism as she could dredge up—the obvious senselessness and fortuity of Callos' murder, the confusion of the police methods, the coincidence—trying to build up a picture of a *muddle* that would soon be cleared up, leaving them free as air. But once by herself there was no dodging the pattern into which events were being forced: she and Mrs. Erskine—or rather, *she*, Lydia —had been under suspicion from the moment that they arrived in Nauplia; under such serious suspicion that the police had at once replaced their driver with one of their own men, and then when he had been killed they had at once suspected—*assumed*, rather—that she, Lydia, had had some connection with it. And not only the police . . . she remembered suddenly Marius Blunt's stony face as he stepped around her in the police station that morning. Against this background Callos' murder could no longer be regarded as fortuitous. There were forces of violence gathering around them . . .

At this point Lydia's thoughts had become so unpleasant that she had jumped up and wandered into the church, looking for something—anything—to distract her eye and mind. It was cold and dingy inside; lumps of plaster had fallen onto the rug that ran from the door to the altar, and there was nothing to look at. But then, turning away disappointed, she had caught sight of Monsieur

Touret's handiwork over the doorway, and she was so absorbed in it that the slow footsteps on the stone stairway and then on the terrace, though she heard them, conveyed no warning to her mind until they were just outside the door of the church. In that instant, as though a map had been flashed onto the wall of her mind, she realized that the only way out of the church was along the terrace—and at once the map disappeared and a picture of Callos' body lying in the trunk of the car appeared in its place.

Marius Blunt's bony face peering around the door was a definite anticlimax, almost a disappointment. For a moment Lydia had thought that she was going to *know*. But instead there was only the old feeling of resentment, and then, welling up, a hot new embarrassment as she remembered that bony cracking sound.

"Hello." He didn't seem surprised or put out to find her. "Isn't . . . isn't it a heavenly day?" There was a pause. "Didn't you—" he went on. "That is, I believe you came to some of my lectures. I'm sure I remember your face. Isn't that right?"

Lydia said slowly, "Yes. Yes, I did."

"I knew it! Now which ones was it you came to?"

"Greek Bronze Age. Summer term."

"Not Homeric Archaeology?"

"No, that clashed with something Roman."

"Ah. Yes, well, I remember now. Last year."

"No, six years ago." Patiently. "Just after your first dig at Mycenae."

He glowed. "Oh, yes, yes, of course. Oh, that's splendid." His pleasure was really quite disproportionate.

"Miss Barnett"—a deep breath—"I'm afraid there has been a really awful muddle of some kind, and I am most terribly sorry about—about what happened this morning."

"Oh. Oh, well. I . . ."

"No. I really must apologize most sincerely."

"Oh, well, that's . . ." Lydia gestured nervously, and her handbag, weighted with the guidebook, swung forward and struck Blunt heavily on the upper leg.

"*Oh!* I'm so sorry."

"Not at all."

Another pause.

"Let us go outside," he said at last, his face still twisted with pain, "and sit down somewhere."

In silence they sat down on the bench with the view of orange trees and the harbor and the hills. Putting her bag down carefully out of harm's way, Lydia said, "Mr. Blunt, there are several things I would like to know. May I ask you?"

"Please." He was all civility.

"How did you in fact discover that I came to your lectures six years ago?"

"But I . . ."

"I know you don't remember my face."

"Well, I see. No. In fact I'm bound to admit that your Mrs.—Erskine, is it? She told me." A faint smile passed across his face. " 'Told' is one word. I went just now to have a drink on the Belle France terrace, and Mrs. Erskine walked over to my table and said, 'You don't know me, but I'm traveling with Lydia Barnett, and I should just like to tell you that you behaved like a real louse to her this morning.' "

"Good gracious!" Lydia was too delighted to feel embarrassment.

"Then she said, 'An educated girl like that takes the trouble to go and listen to your classes and you can't even help her out when the police pull her in for questioning.' Or words to that effect."

"Goodness. What did *you* say?"

"Nothing much. I agreed with her, really. I'd already realized by that time that the police had got it wrong. But Mrs. Erskine gave me what I needed—confirmation, I mean."

Lydia looked at him curiously. "You mean that if I'd been to your lectures I couldn't have been responsible for Callos' murder?"

"Well, not exactly, but—" Blunt stirred awkwardly on the bench. "Well, yes, since you put it that way. It *does* after all prove that they've got the wrong person."

Leaning back, Lydia closed her eyes and laughed helplessly.

"I wonder," she said at last, reaching for a hankerchief, "what Major Papandros would say to that as an item of proof."

Blunt looked uncomfortable. "Well, actually I did ring him up as soon as Mrs. Erskine told me, and he wasn't altogether—happy about it."

"I should think not!" But after all, he had tried to put things right at once, whatever his evidence. . . . "That was good of you, though. You seem to be very in with the police," she went on cautiously. "You're not Scotland Yard or anything are you?" Joke.

"No, but it's all my period, of course."

"Your period?"

"Yes. If they find anything, they'll want an opinion on whether it's genuine or not."

Lydia floundered. "What on earth are you talking about?"

He was clearly much surprised. "The Adelmann finds."

"Adelmann? Tiryns? Oh, *no*—I thought you were in their confidence somehow on all this business of Callos and the police and their suspicions of me."

"Yes, well, that's what all this is."

"Do you mean," she said slowly, "that Callos was mixed up with the Adelmann things in some way?"

"Not Callos himself, he was a—"

"A soldier."

"Policeman, actually. But, yes, he was keeping an eye on you because they think you're a courier."

"Courier?"

Blunt rubbed a hand over his eyes. "I'm sorry. I'm starting in the middle. I've thought about nothing else for six weeks, and I've got to the stage of forgetting"—he gestured apologetically—"that there are people who aren't so involved. But I think you really ought to have the full story—you may be going to need it . . . if things go on like this?"

"Please."

"Okay." He sat for a moment collecting his thoughts, and then a faint, self-mocking smile passed across his face. "I will endeavor to be brief." He cleared his throat and started briskly. "As I told you yesterday, it seems very likely that in 1892 Dietrich Adelmann made some valuable discoveries—probably of golden treasure of some kind—at Tiryns and concealed them somewhere in this area. *If* he left any information in writing as to their whereabouts it would have been in letters to his wife, whom he had recently married and to whom he wrote every day. But unfortunately these letters have never been available to scholars. The shock of her husband's death finally capsized the poor woman's reason—it had never, I gather, been tremendously stable—and within a few months she was shut up in a home in Switzerland, and all her belongings, including the papers, were seized by the Swiss authorities and held in trust for her. Though mad, however, she was also extremely healthy and lived to be ninety-one, dying only at the end of last year.

"Now, the discovery of a really significant hoard of Bronze Age objects from Tiryns could"—Blunt made sweeping gestures with both arms—"it could *double* our knowledge of the period. So there have always been plenty of scholars—archaeologists, people like me—very interested in Mrs. Adelmann and her papers, and it was generally believed that at her death the papers would be made available to bona fide researchers—and of course to the Greek authorities. Perhaps this was just wishful thinking. But anyway, it was quite a bombshell when, at the beginning of this year, it was found that her will left everything—*everything*—to her son Gustav, who had emigrated to America and died there in 1923. After a further delay, it was discovered that *his* will had left everything to his wife—or rather, widow—and she couldn't be traced. *So*, that was how things stood at the end of January. Two and a half months ago . . ."

Blunt leaned forward and sighed. "I suppose we should have foreseen it." He seemed for the moment to have forgotten Lydia, and the story. "Someone should have thought . . ."

"Two and a half months ago?"

Blunt roused himself, but he started on quite a different tack. "Really rich Americans are a breed apart, you know. They have to spend their money somehow, and once you've got everything, only scarcity creates value." He stopped and tried again. "As you know, the vogue for archaeology in the States has almost passed all bounds. I'm not talking about scholars—their scholars have always been interested—but about collectors, millionaires who are tired of the Impressionists and want something different. And once you have demand, you have supply. The price of genuine prehistoric objects had gone up in

New York—oh, fifty times, I should say, in the last twenty years. The trouble is, there are so few really definitely genuine things available. So there are now masses of forgeries —and there is also an increasing number of thefts from museums and from archaeological sites. And, in brief, one of the shadier New York dealers let it be known early this year that he could get three million dollars for whatever it was that Adelmann had found—"

Blunt broke off at Lydia's exclamation and laughed. "Oh, yes, there's that sort of money in America—for a really conspicuous bit of consumption. And in the first place, he would give a million dollars and no questions asked to whoever delivered the Adelmann finds to New York—what's wrong?"

"It wasn't really the *amount* of money that surprised me. But when you say that a dealer thought he could get three million dollars for the finds—wouldn't they belong to the Greek government? I mean, how could he sell them?"

"They couldn't be auctioned at Sotheby's, if that's what you mean." Blunt grinned faintly. "But there are other ways of making a sale in the art world. Suppose some Mycenaean objects turned up in the States in the possession of a well-known collector. There would be no proof that they were the Adelmann finds because no one has ever seen them. But the collector would know, and so would the rest of the world—*and* the Greek government—that that's what they were. So, just to finish off the story, the inevitable happened. You will, I am sure, say that it *was* inevitable, that we should have foreseen it, should have taken precautions—" He turned to Lydia earnestly.

"But tell me," Lydia said gently, "what happened."

"What? Oh, well, all the Adelmann papers were stolen from the office in Switzerland where they were being held while the question of inheritance was sorted out. On the first day of March. Six weeks ago."

"Golly," said Lydia, for whom the pattern of events was at last beginning to come clear.

Blunt was cheered by her reaction. "Gnashing of teeth," he said, waving his arms. "Beating of breasts, sackcloth the fashionable wear. The world of scholarship and the Greek police indulging in an orgy of mutual self-recrimination. Me in despair," he added quietly. "It seemed to us all quite clear that whoever had got the papers would simply come to Greece, pick the stuff up, fly it straight to New York and feed it into the system. And that would be that. No one would ever see it again, and I would never be able to test my theory about the cultural influences of the . . . *Anyway,*" he said, recalling himself with visible effort, "the Greek police put themselves on a full alert, and so did the customs, but without a great deal of hope. And then, suddenly, a week ago today, the police had an extraordinary piece of luck. A house had been broken into in Nauplia and they hauled a chap in for questioning—a minor criminal, well known to the police. He usually sticks to Athens, so his mere presence in Nauplia was enough to make them suspicious. As soon as they started questioning him it became clear that he had a perfectly good alibi for the housebreaking, but also that he was mixed up in something else and was extremely nervous about it. In the end they made a deal with him by which he went free in return for telling them all that he knew—which wasn't much, unfortunately, but it *was* significant, very significant. . . . And now I want you to listen very carefully to this."

"I'm listening," Lydia said mildly.

Blunt said slowly, "He said that his instructions were to wait in Nauplia for an English lady who was coming to get the Adelmann treasures. He was to give her any help she needed. She would be traveling"—Blunt had slowed to a sort of dictation speed—"as companion to an American lady. That's all he knew."

In the silence that followed, the noises of the town, rising faintly in the afternoon warmth, were suddenly obtrusive and distracting. Lydia shifted herself on the bench, looking to right and left as though for escape.

"All right . . . all right. But that still doesn't mean I did it."

"No, and I *know* you didn't. But you must admit"—he glanced at her apologetically—"that you must have seemed pretty obvious to the police. And you didn't help, either. The only place you showed the slightest interest in was Tiryns. You couldn't wait even a day."

"Okay," said Lydia harshly, feeling her anger, illogically, start to build up against him, "so the police think I'm here to get the Adelmann treasures."

"Not only the police."

"Who else?"

"Whoever killed Callos."

Lydia turned and stared at him.

"They wanted your car so badly they were prepared to indulge in violence to get it. I can only think," he said, looking at her meditatively, "that once again it was your curious behavior yesterday. You did behave very oddly, you know, going off alone to Tiryns, and then going back after dark with Callos and the car. They must have been *so* sure you'd got the treasures, they just had to take any risk to get the car and search it."

Suddenly, astonishingly, he smiled broadly. "Which is, you will admit, a great bit of luck."

"Luck?"

He started to tick off points on his fingers. "They've come out into the open, so we know they're here. We also know that they haven't got the treasures yet, which in turn suggests that they don't yet know where they are, which means that we may yet be able to stop them from getting them. We're considerably further on than we were twenty-four hours ago."

"Yes, but who are 'they'?"

"Ah, now that *is* the question. There may be several different groups, of course. I have a little theory—"

"This Englishwoman," Lydia said thoughtfully, "the one who's coming to get the treasures according to the man the police picked up, what about her? Aren't there any known English criminals—female ones—who would fit the bill? Wouldn't that give the police a lead?"

"If I may say so"—he looked at her with clear admiration—"it is a very great pleasure to have to do with a trained mind. Indeed, that *is* the best lead we have, and it is, as it happens, on that point that I base my theory. Have you heard of the Firenze gang? No? Well, do you remember reading in the papers about a theft of Renaissance bronzes in Florence, about a year ago? That was the first time they really got into the news, but they've been active for some time. They specialize in thefts from museums. Not quite Topkapi level, perhaps, but some very extraordinary feats. The Florence job, for example, involved the theft of more than fifty bronzes from three different rooms in the museum *while* the museum was open and *while* there were three attendants on duty—who noticed nothing. Highly professional, in fact. There's an Englishwoman involved with them—indeed, she's probably the moving spirit. *I* think it's very likely she—"

"But the police don't?"

"Oh, they have all sorts of objections—that the Bologna lot have never operated outside Italy, that they don't have any Americans in with them and the chap they questioned said definitely that she'd be traveling as companion to an *American* woman. Anyway, the question is on ice now, as far as the police are concerned."

"Why on ice?"

"Because they see no need to look further than you—you fit all the requirements."

"Oh. Oh, I see. . . . Well, I hope it *is* the Florence lot."

"Do you? So that I can have the pleasure of being right? That's nice of you. But I'm not so sure that I want them around, actually. They're a nasty lot. This Englishwoman who works with them, they call her La Gioconda because she smiles all the time—especially when she's watching torture."

"Torture?"

"Well, to extract information, or punish suspected informers—you saw what had been done to Callos—that sort of thing. That's one reason why I think it's her lot who are active around here now."

"Is she . . . mad?"

"Probably. Her father shot himself, or so they say, rather than sell his collection of paintings to meet the death duties on his estate, and after that of course everything had to be sold. So now she collects in a more . . . unorthodox way. Unbalanced, certainly. But very sane where theft and violence are concerned. And that, by the way, is why I'm not going to press your innocence with Papandros. As long as the police are watching you, you're comparatively safe from the others."

"Watching me?"

"Go and look." He jerked his head in the direction of the stone steps.

Lydia went reluctantly to the end of the terrace. As she appeared at the top of the steps, two small boys stopped playing and stared up at her curiously. But a man leaning against the house opposite with his hat tilted over his eyes didn't move.

"I see." Lydia sat down again meekly on the bench.

"You see, the—other chaps won't necessarily be put off by finding nothing in your car."

"No," said Lydia slowly, "no they won't. Mrs. Erskine found a boy going through her luggage this morning."

"Mrs. Erskine, now." Blunt jumped at the lead. "What, er, what about her?" He tried to sound casual, but without success.

"Mrs. Erskine? Surely you don't think—"

"I think nothing. I only wonder. Tell me about her."

"Well, born and brought up in Iowa. Husband edits a newspaper. Never been out of the States before."

"How did you find her?"

"She found me. She wrote to the Congress of Women Graduates in London. I was at college with the secretary. Surely the police don't think that she—"

"Lydia, once and for all"—*Lydia?*—"the police are concentrating on *you* at the moment. Papandros isn't even bothering to make inquiries about anyone else."

"Oh, I see. And what will you tell him about our conversation this afternoon?"

"Well, that—" He blinked. "That though you have twice today offered me physical violence there doesn't seem to be anything else suspicious about your behavior."

"Oh . . . oh—" Suddenly she started to laugh, feeling immensely and irrationally cheerful. "Very fair, as you would say, very pretty."

"Quits?"

"Quits." *Surely*, she thought, *we're not going to go on shaking hands every time we meet?* But this time there was a difference.

"You're a *good* girl," he said with sudden warmth, and still holding her hand, he bent forward and kissed her cheek.

He was clearly just as surprised as she was. "Ah . . . *lilies*," he said, jumping up to examine a gasoline can full of tobacco flowers. "Very early this year. Are you a gardener?"

"Not really." *And that would seem to go for you too.*

But then, rousing herself to cover up his embarrassment, she took him off to see the church, and Monsieur Touret's memorial, and by the time they strolled back down the steps and past the motionless figure with the hat tilted over his eyes, Blunt had recovered himself entirely and was telling her happily about Turkish naval tactics at the battle of Navarino.

Lydia didn't recover so quickly. The kiss had been one more shock than she could take—in a day of shocks. By the time she got back to the hotel she was feeling decidedly shaky.

Mrs. Erskine, sitting on her bed with her feet up and her face covered with grease, welcomed her gaily.

"I've started!" she cried, indicating a bottle of Scotch and a glass on the bedside table. "I've decided we should both start on the booze and stay on it until all this business clears up."

This was so clearly a departure from the habits and principles of a lifetime that Lydia felt obliged to react suitably.

"I have never," she said, pouring a serious quantity of Scotch into a glass for herself, "heard of such depravity. Not in the whole of my life."

One of the endearing peculiarities of the Belle France was that every room contained at least three beds. Now Lydia established herself on a spare one near the window and kicked off her shoes.

"I came to Nauplia to be quiet and relax," Mrs. Erskine went on, "and they kill my driver and try to steal my clothes, and then you tell me that the driver was really a policeman, and finally they won't even let us leave town." She waved her glass. "It's crazy."

Lydia glanced unobtrusively at the bottle, but the level was still high; Mrs. Erskine had merely been thinking about things.

And things were even crazier than Mrs. Erskine thought. . . . But Lydia decided suddenly to say nothing about what Blunt had just told her—partly because she wanted first to mull it over by herself and partly too because he had succeeded in making her wonder about Mrs. Erskine. Looking at that candid greasy face, it was impossible to believe Mrs. Erskine capable of an evil thought, let alone an evil deed. But the fact remained that Lydia knew nothing at all about her background beyond what Mrs. Erskine herself had told her.

It *was* odd that Mrs. Erskine had insisted on coming to Nauplia, and odd too that she as well as Lydia seemed to be attracting so much attention—and violence. There was one way of checking quickly on her story, but Lydia shrank from it.

"Your date called," said Mrs. Erskine suddenly. "He'll pick you up at eight."

"My *date?*"

"Henry James. He said you're having dinner with him tonight."

"Oh, but that's nonsense. I told him I couldn't."

"Oh, now, Lydia, he's a nice boy. I think you should go. You must have some fun on this trip."

"But I don't want to." *I don't want to leave you, and not only because you're my employer.*

"Now don't worry about me. I've already said I'll eat dinner with that nice Mr. Blunt"—*Oh!*—"I spoke to him while you were out this afternoon."

"Yes, he told me."

"Oh, you've seen him, then? He was very charming."

So charming, apparently, that Mrs. Erskine had now forgotten how their conversation had started. And he'd asked Mrs. Erskine out to dinner. *He might at least have told me.*

"That's why I'm having a little rest now. I don't want to be too sleepy at dinnertime." And grease on the face and all. Blunt must really have gone to town.

"Okay then, I may as well dine with Henry."

"That's right, dear. Put on something pretty."

In the bath Lydia contrived to avoid analyzing her disappointment at the thought of a delicious dinner tête-à-tête with Henry while Mrs. Erskine was dining with Blunt . . . with Marius. . . . But her own evening with Henry would of course be Great Fun.

"Lydia, I'm off." Mrs. Erskine tapped lightly on the bathroom door. "Have a lovely time with Henry."

Have a really beastly time with Marius. Oh, don't be so absurd.

"And you too," she called back warmly.

In her room again, she stood quite still and looked at

herself in the mirror on the wardrobe door. She was wearing a long green kimono, and with her dark hair pinned
up on her head she looked for a moment exotic and un-
familiar, but even so not like a girl who would . . .

Tightening her sash, she stepped onto the balcony.
Three more steps, and she was in Mrs. Erskine's room.
She knew exactly where to look. The white dressing case
was lying on the writing table, and it was unlocked; Mrs.
Erskine had yet to acquire the habits of suspicion.

The passport was new, and the only stamps were those
of London Airport a week ago and Athens the day before
yesterday. *Marthe Lucy Engen Erskine. Birthdate—April
24, 1906.* That made her fifty-nine now. If she married at
nineteen, that made it 1925; her daughter might have
been born the next year—yes, it was all possible. *Birth
place—Iowa. Hair . . . Eyes . . . Height. . . .* All as
it should be. Under the passport was the bundle of letters that had been waiting for Mrs. Erskine at the Bourtzi,
airmail envelopes with red, white and blue edges.

*Darling Mom, It seems like an age since you left. We
all enjoyed your letter from London so much. Polly called
Friday and I told her . . . the P.T.A. meeting . . .
Janie's boyfriend . . . looked in at the house like you said
. . . everything fine . . . Pa writing real soon . . . the
garden. . . . Dear Granma, The cashmere sweater arrived
yesterday. It's darling! . . . Peter . . . Gerry . . . Herb . . .
gorgeous . . . Herb. . . . Dear Mom, I guess you must
wonder why you haven't heard . . . the office . . . trip . . .
the boys . . .*

Nothing, nothing, nothing that shouldn't have been
there. And everything exactly as Mrs. Erskine had told
her. Lydia stumped back along the terrace, raging. *So
now what have you proved? She tells the truth and you
don't.*

But it was after eight, and she must snap out of it. Her
dress was new, coral-colored and exquisite, and it didn't
soothe her in the very slightest. Low-heeled coral shoes,
a small black bag, no jewelry. *Not bad,* she conceded at
last, glaring at herself in the mirror. Then she picked up
her fluffy white coat and went down to flatten Henry.

Henry didn't flatten easily.

"Hi," he said absently, pulling out a chair for her at
his table. "Would you like a drink? No? Okay, then, let's

go. I thought we'd eat at the Xenia. Up on the hill. Nice view. Perhaps"—he looked vaguely at the fragile coral pumps—"perhaps you'd better change your shoes."

"Certainly *not!*" Lydia was astonished at her own vehemence. "We'll go by taxi."

Henry was unsurprised. "Okay," he said meekly, casting her a single *Et tu, Brute* look, and snapped his fingers for the waiter.

The Xenia straddled the ridge of rock above the town, and there were views both ways—down onto the bay and the fort, and out on the other side of the headland toward the open sea. It was built of glass and steel, and there were carpets and bellboys and plashing fountains with green plants in pots and sifting, drifting groups of tourists, dazed and somnambulistic. Except for the view, it could have been anywhere.

Lydia, guiltily, felt soothed. This was a phony world with no real existence in time or space, but it was safe and predictable, and she was wearing the right clothes. Major Papandros had no place here, nor sudden death, nor spying on one's friends . . .

Among the potted plants they came suddenly upon Bubi and Annie sipping martinis. They too looked depressed. Henry tried to slip past, but Bubi caught sight of them immediately.

"Ah, Miss Barnett!" he cried, jumping to his feet. "What a pleasure." He nodded briefly to Henry. "But I'm not sure if you have met Miss Ollenshaw—our guide, companion and good friend."

Annie, looking sour, extended a bony hand.

"Yes, indeed," said Lydia pleasantly. "We met briefly this afternoon."

"Ah, then you are friends already!" Annie's expression repudiated the charge. "Won't you join us? Sit here, Miss Barnett. What will you drink?"

Lydia, hoping to avoid entanglement, glanced toward Henry. But he, a rabbit confronting a snake, had already sunk down miserably beside Annie, who now addressed him.

"I'll have another," she said.

Henry got to his feet again and went in search of a waiter.

It occurred to Lydia that she had yet to hear Annie speak except to issue a direct command.

"And are you enjoying Greece, Miss Ollenshaw?" she asked, experimenting.

But Bubi intervened at once, as though high words had been exchanged.

"We are all of us," he said emolliently, "depressed by the delays imposed on us. The cameramen, you know, with their union, and the extras, with *their* union, and of course the authorities are so hopeless, with all their regulations, all their *red tape* . . ."

Henry returned, shortly followed by a waiter with four martinis, and for a moment there was silence. Lydia started to feel depressed again; the anxieties and frustrations of the outside world couldn't, it seemed, be held at bay indefinitely by wall-to-wall carpeting. However, there was such a thing as social duty. She roused herself to another effort.

But Annie was before her.

"Well," she said in her flat, American voice, "nice seeing you."

Not a comment, a command. *An unbroken record,* reflected Lydia with admiration, as Henry sprang to his feet and mumbled the most formal of excuses.

Bubi, looking apologetic, held Lydia's hand as she said good-bye. "Miss Barnett, another time we will have a longer chat."

"Quite a character, Annie," said Lydia guardedly, as the headwaiter steered them through the maze of tables.

"God, she's hell," said Henry passionately. "She never speaks except to tell you to do something—well, you saw. And Bubi just sort of laughs. We have to have a woman, apparently, because Mary-Lou's under age, but Bubi might have got someone a bit more . . . possible. *And* she leaves the galley of the *Arcady* like a stockyard. It'll take me weeks to get it clean."

Gloomily they sat down opposite each other, with the sea far away below them behind a wall of glass. Henry sighed deeply. "Vichyssoise is nice," he said sepulchrally, "and this is the one place you can get a decent steak. But would you rather—" He stared helplessly at the enormous menu.

But Lydia was feeling ashamed of her bad temper earlier in the evening.

"That sounds lovely, Henry."

"Okay. Well, then, burgundy or claret?"

"Oh, no, you choose. I'm sure you know best." *Steady now, don't overdo it.*

But Henry brightened visibly.

"Well, now, let's see." He tut-tutted through the red wines. "Perhaps we should try a Greek one." Prolonged consultations with the waiter, an eventual decision.

Then, deprived of action, he leaned his elbows on the table and stared out despondently at the darkening sea. It was gradually being borne in on Lydia that Henry had troubles other than his dislike of Annie.

"How's the film?" she asked sympathetically.

"What? Oh, well, that's all still in suspense, really. There's, you see—" He hitched his chair forward and lowered his voice. "Actually, Bubi has some, er, business interests in Greece too. And that's what's on his mind at the moment."

"And those aren't going too well?"

"No. No, they're not."

Pause. Henry sighed deeply.

"Lydia, do you know any Greek? No, of course you wouldn't."

Lydia shut her mouth again.

"It's really crazy," he said somberly, "and damned inefficient, too."

"What is?"

"Well, look. When Bubi took me on, it was mainly because he wanted the yacht, but he also asked me if I knew Greek. He didn't want me to speak it or anything, but just to be able to read the characters and pick out names of places and so on. So I said yes. Well"—he paused and leaned back to allow the vichyssoise to come to rest in front of him—"I'd done a bit at school—school cert and so on. So I thought I'd manage, and anyway, I needed the job because, well, just at that time I needed the job rather badly." He ducked his head and started to drink the soup. "Then, when we got here he showed me this message from his—his contact, you know, giving the names of places for—well, for meetings. So I told Bubi what it said. But the places were all very peculiar, and now it turns out that half of them don't exist at all. It's not my fault, but Bubi's livid and he's threatening to sack me."

"I'm so sorry." The soup was good.

"Yes, well, so I said why not ring up your contact, or write, or something? But now he says he's got no way of getting in touch with him at all. Beyond this crazy message."

"So the yacht *is* yours, Henry?"

"Well, yes. But don't tell Bubi I told you. He likes to pretend she's his. I—I charter her generally, you know. Parties of people. Sicily and Stromboli and all that."

"I see. But, Henry, these Greek places—what do you mean when you say 'peculiar'?"

"Well, some of them are all right. Argos, for instance. It's quite a big town. And Hermione's a sizable village. But some of them aren't really places at all. Not even villages. Asiné, for example—"

"Asiné!"

"Yes, do you know it? It's just a hump. Down by the sea. Bubi went off there several times last week."

"What were the other places?" asked Lydia casually, but her head was whirling. Bubi with *business interests* at Asiné . . . at a deserted Mycenaean site.

"Oh, I can't remember them all. Troy something. That's where they'd been trying when they came back yesterday."

"But Troy's over in Asia Minor."

"Is it? Well, anyway, now there's just one more place on the list that they haven't tried yet, but it simply *does not exist.*" He spoke with emphasis, as though repeating an argument that had already taken place several times. "Eionai. I can't produce it out of thin air." His voice was plaintive.

Something—the vaguest memory—stirred in Lydia's mind. "But Bubi wants you to find it?"

"Not only *wants.* He says if I can't find it I can take myself and the yacht and, er, go off, and I can whistle for the rest of what he owes me."

"Oh, goodness, Henry, what a mess." Lydia kept her face down as she talked, fiddling with her glass, trying to think. "But I'm sure it'll all be all right, you know." Desperately she began to talk about other things.

"Henry, I found such an amusing place this afternoon.

A church with a memorial to the foreign soldiers—the non-Greeks, you know—who were killed in the war of independence." If Bubi and Asiné were connected, then Bubi and that battered dead body might be connected—and Henry too. Honest, bumbling Henry. "All so amateur and funny. You must go and see it. And such pretty flowers and . . ."

It was uphill work. Henry didn't want to be amused, and Lydia, her mind elsewhere, was aware of sounding sillier and sillier as she dredged for things to say. But she kept it going until well past the steak and the sticky honey cakes. Then, when the waiter had brought the tiny cups of sweet, strong, gritty coffee, there was suddenly just nothing more to say.

"I do think you might be more sympathetic about my job." Henry sounded deeply hurt.

Lydia avoided his eye. "I seem to have heard of Eionai," she mumbled at last, despite herself.

"Have you really?"

"But I can't think where."

"Well. I'll just have to try for another charter, I suppose. Difficult at short notice. . . . We may as well go," he added bleakly, after a while. "No point in sitting here."

But as they walked down the hill he suddenly tucked his arm through Lydia's. "It's been so nice talking to you. You've quite cheered me up."

Lydia repressed the desire to snatch her arm away. "Well," she said lamely. "I'm sorry I haven't been more help."

"Oh, no, you've been *very* kind—I say, look at that. Isn't that super?" He stopped at the top of a long flight of steps and gazed at the black bay and the string of lights along the quay. Twenty yards behind them other footsteps stopped abruptly.

"Isn't she lovely?" It was the *Arcady*, of course, that had caught Henry's eye, gleaming white under the lights at the mast head.

"Gorgeous." There was, of course, no way of knowing it was the police. She detached herself from Henry and moved on quickly down the steps.

"If you remember anything about Eionai," said Henry, catching up with her, "you will tell me, won't you?"

"Oh, yes, Henry, of course."

On the terrace of the Belle France they came upon Marius and Mrs. Erskine, their heads confidingly close together.

A curious sound was audible, and, suddenly Henry laughed.

"*Home, James, and don't spare the horses*—oh, jolly good! Isn't that your Mrs. Erskine?"

So Marius and Mrs. Erskine had been singing musical comedy songs together . . .

Marius, unusually presentable in a dark suit, sprang to his feet and pulled up more chairs. Lydia introduced Henry.

"Oh, my." Mrs. Erskine was wiping away tears of laughter with a tiny lace handkerchief. "I never thought I'd meet any young people who knew that song! We thought it was corny when I was a girl. Did you have a good time, dear? I just don't seem to have stopped laughing all evening." Fondly she gazed at Marius. "Mr. Blunt's real *folksy*."

Lydia hoped that Marius would curl up with embarrassment, but he was clearly delighted. "But I've hardly started on my repertoire," he protested. "What about—"

"No, no, *really!*" cried Mrs. Erskine. "We mustn't start again tonight. It's far too late. Tomorrow, though . . ." She turned to Lydia. "Mr. Blunt has asked me to go with him to Mycenae tomorrow morning. Isn't that kind? Now that we"—she paused delicately, glancing at Henry—"don't have the car anymore . . ."

Even if one didn't want to go, it would have been nice to be asked, thought Lydia—especially as one did want to go.

"Well, good night then." Marius was on his feet. "What a splendid evening! Mrs. Erskine, thank you so very much."

"Oh, no, Mr. Blunt, it's . . ."

I must tell him about Henry and Bubi, thought Lydia. But he was gone, disappearing briskly around the corner of the hotel in the direction of the King Otto.

Lydia's first thought the next morning was to find Marius quickly.

It wasn't difficult. He was on the terrace having breakfast with Mrs. Erskine.

"I was just explaining to Mr. Blunt," began Mrs. Erskine without preliminaries, "that we in the Midwest are really in the front line now."

"Oh?"

"In a nuclear war."

"Oh, I see. Yes. Well, I suppose you are." Lydia poured herself some coffee. "That must be a tremendous comfort to you. I personally can't imagine anything worse than surviving a nuclear war. I'd be so bad at life afterwards—living in caves and things and hunting wild animals, cooking over an open fire." Mrs. Erskine was looking thoughtful, but Marius didn't seem to be listening. She appealed to him directly. "What do *you* think?"

"What?" He spoke absently. "Oh . . . I suppose I'd just move into college."

Lydia glanced at him sharply. He was hunched over the table, thoughtfully examining the alluvial deposit in the bottom of his coffee cup. And there was no possible way of deciding if he was serious. Mrs. Erskine continued to talk about fallout. Lydia gave up and buttered her toast.

"Come along, Lydia." Marius stood up abruptly. "Race you to the end of the quay."

Lydia stared.

"Run along, dear," said Mrs. Erskine genially. "Stretch your legs."

"Certainly *not!*" But then, catching up with his idea, she added hastily, "Okay, okay," and set off at a ladylike trot, cursing under her breath. Fortunately it was still too early for the inscrutable black-suited gentlemen. Marius loped along beside her, drawing ahead only at the very end modestly to register his victory.

"Well, that was a bit elaborate."

"Puff, puff."

"And what's the excitement?"

"Mrs. Erskine's okay." They had reached a long stone breakwater jutting out into the bay, and now Marius sat down and dangled his espadrilles toward the turquoise water. "The police did a check with Iowa over last night. That's what I came to tell you. Everything she said to you is right."

"Well, that's nice." Lydia sat down beside him, spreading out her skirt.

"It might still be interesting to look at her passport. But as that's not possible—"

"That's been done."

Marius stared. "Our own Mata Hari?"

"Yes. And don't laugh. I'm very ashamed. But now listen to me."

Rapidly she told him about Henry. Marius listened carefully without interrupting.

"My God, you're right, you know," he said finally. "How extraordinary. What were those places?"

"Asiné. Troy. Hermione. Then one that he said didn't exist—Eionai, I think."

"Well." He squinted out across the dazzling water of the harbor. "Eionai certainly doesn't exist anymore. But it might be a code, I suppose. Come on, we must go." He stood up and hauled her to her feet.

"Where?"

"Your favorite man."

"Not *Papandros?*"

"I'm afraid so."

"Oh, Marius, must we?"

"Now, Lydia—be sensible. Who else can we possibly go to?"

"Okay." Lydia sighed.

"Good girl. Come on."

They dived into the maze of streets and threaded their way across the town. The police station was revealed as a pleasant building with green shutters and good proportions, but Lydia felt a reminiscent chill as they clattered in and started up the stairs.

Major Papandros was civil but unwelcoming. He would be delighted, as at any time, to talk to Mr. Blunt. He would prefer just at the moment not to see Miss Barnett, but Mr. Blunt might speak to him alone if he wished.

Marius was unexpectedly firm.

"Major Papandros, I would really be most grateful if you would listen to me. Miss Barnett has some information that I believe is extremely relevant. I will talk to you alone afterwards if you want me to."

After a moment Papandros shrugged. "Very well."

"This is what has happened." Rapidly, Marius repeated what Lydia had told him, referring to her from time to time for confirmation. "That's right, Lydia, isn't it?

"It seems to me," he concluded, "that this Benedict man is after the Adelmann treasure. He clearly has some lead as to where the stuff is, but he can't understand the messages properly. If you arrest him quickly"—he was really quite excited now—"you can prevent his getting to the stuff *and,* with any luck, you'll get the information on which he's working."

Major Papandros hadn't moved. He sat sideways in his chair, one booted leg flung over the arm, tapping softly on his desk with a long ivory paper knife. His face remained blank.

"Is that all you have to say to me, Mr. Blunt?" he asked after a short silence.

"Well, yes, but isn't that more than—"

"Mr. Blunt." Papandros was suddenly amused. "Do you really imagine that I would have taken no steps to investigate so curious a collection of, er, visitors to Greece as Mr. Benedict and his friends? Especially with a yacht? And just at this moment? Have you come to tell me that the sun is shining out of doors?"

Marius was taken aback.

"Well, I didn't mean that you wouldn't have. But this is surely *evidence*—something more than just suspicion."

"Mr. Blunt, I'm afraid you are starting to see the Adelmann treasures under every stone. There *are* other reasons for coming to Greece, even if you are coming illicitly." He stood up and strolled around the desk. "I am in the unhappy position this morning of finding myself"—he paused, feeling for the right phrase—"back where I started. I have no suspects." There was a flash of white teeth. "Not even Miss Barnett."

Lydia's eyebrows rose.

"London confirms everything that you have said about yourself." He fingered the telegrams on his desk with evident disappointment. "But Mr. Benedict won't do, I'm afraid, as an alternative."

"You're sure?"

"Sure." There was a pause, filled with tension. To Lydia's surprise, it was Major Papandros who gave way.

"Miss Barnett's friend, Mr. James," he went on reluctantly, "is wanted by the Italian authorities on seven charges. Of smuggling. Cigarettes. He is"—he paused again—"small-time. Definitely small-time."

"And Benedict?" prompted Marius, startled.

"Mr. Benedict is slightly *larger*-time, I should say. Not yet quite *big*-time, but certainly—larger." He was enjoying himself now, dodging the issue. But Lydia realized suddenly that he was going to tell them.

"Not cigarettes, in his case. Americans coming to Greece buy theirs on the plane, and the natives prefer our own kind. So there is no market here for smuggled cigarettes. But whiskey, now, that is another matter. Even in this land of ouzo, there is, I am sorry to say, a constant market for whiskey, and as the Greek import duties on whiskey are very high, the possibilities of profit for the—duty-free importer, shall we say?—are very considerable. Do you begin to see, Mr. Blunt? Asiné may be, as you say, an odd place to have ordinary business interests, but for Mr. Benedict's particular business it would be ideal. As Miss Barnett"—his eyes slid around to Lydia—"will no doubt agree."

"I?" Lydia was surprised. "I don't know Asiné."

"You and I were there together yesterday morning, Miss Barnett."

"Asiné! That beach?"

"Well, it is the hill above the beach that is Asiné itself."

"I . . . I had no idea."

"And the other places—the less well known they are, the better for the purposes of Mr. Benedict and his friends. This 'Troy,' for example, that Mr. James mentioned. That will no doubt be Troizen, another early site, about fifty-five miles from here, also near the sea, also very deserted."

"I see." Marius was subdued. "Aren't you going to arrest them, then, if you know what they're doing?"

"But they haven't *done anything*, Mr. Blunt! Nor will they." Major Papandros smiled briefly. "It has been really most unfortunate for Mr. Benedict and his friends that they should arrive in Nauplia at just this moment. As you will no doubt have observed, every person—or parcel—leaving or entering the yacht is carefully checked by officers of the customs service, an unusual precaution that is popularly believed to be linked in some way with our anxieties about the Adelmann trophies. So he has been obliged to investigate a number of possible alternative landing places for his whiskey. Again unfortunately for him, deserted beaches in Greece rarely have a satisfactory motor road running to them, and he has been obliged to reject one after another. Asiné might have served the purpose, but since the—events, shall we say?—of yesterday morning it is too much in the public eye. Tourists are flocking there. And so I suspect that in the end, when Mr. Benedict has really taken in all these facts, he and his friends will sail away, with all those carboard boxes market 'Fragile' still in the hold of his yacht. And I assure you, Mr. Blunt, that we shall do nothing to stop him. And now if you will forgive me, Mr. Blunt, Miss Barnett. There's a lot going on just at present."

"Yes, of course." Marius and Lydia got hastily to their feet.

Major Papandros put a hand on Marius' shoulder as they walked toward the door, "To tell you the truth, I am beginning to doubt very much whether anyone at all is coming after the Adelmann trophies. They are certainly not here yet. And, really, we have enough to do without that. Vandalism at Mycenae—"

"*Vandalism?*"

"Oh, yes. There's always a certain amount in the tourist season, you know, but this seems to be on a more serious scale than usual. People have been breaking in at night."

"I wasn't told anything about this." Marius was indignant. "What happened?"

"Someone has been digging in the grave circle."

"The grave circle? But it's been dug again and again."

"Yes, but this isn't archaeology. They have dug very clumsily. And then they dug up a section of church floor at Argos—right under the dome. Very extraordinary. I say 'they' because it seems to be the same people, though what their purpose is I cannot imagine. But in police work one comes across these lunatics."

He had walked them courteously to the door of the police station. Now he shook hands.

"Good-bye, Miss Barnett. Good-bye Mr. Blunt. And don't worry any more about the irregularities of Mr. Benedict's business life. You can rest assured that we shall not allow him to break the law in any respect."

"Squashed us all flat as kippers," said Marius at last, throwing a small stone into the sea.

"Left us *aussi morts que moutons*," agreed Lydia sadly.

"That is that, I'm afraid."

"Yes. Bubi and Henry are in the clear again. He's an extraordinary man, Papandros, don't you think? Marvelous English, and obviously extremely bright. Isn't that very unusual for a provincial police major?"

Marius grinned gloomily. "Whatever else he is, he's certainly not the provincial police! Papandros was sent from Athens as a special investigator to deal with the Adelmann treasures, and I strongly suspect that on his home ground he's considerably more than a major."

"I see. But now he's saying that he doubts whether anything will happen on the Adelmann thing at all."

"I wouldn't take that too seriously," Marius said slowly. "If he really thought that, he wouldn't still be here— quite apart from Callos—and he certainly wouldn't be worrying about vandalism at Mycenae. Come on," he added suddenly, "I want to see that."

He turned briskly and started back toward the hotel.

"What about Mrs. Erskine?" asked Lydia, breaking into a run to keep up. "You said you'd take her."

"She'll have to wait," said Marius shortly. "This is urgent."

He drove the Vespa like a demon. First the long, straight road through the orange groves, then Argos full of slow-moving pedestrians—Lydia shut her eyes and hung on— then the green and brown plain again with the road crossing and recrossing a railway line, climbing slowly, continuously, mile after mile, and then a railway station, a sign: MYKENE, and a road leading off to the right. A couple of miles farther on, they swept through a small village, the road curved and climbed more steeply between low rocky hills, and then, suddenly, they were there.

"Eccolà!" shouted Marius with a theatrical gesture. The Vespa swerved sharply and recovered itself. Lydia opened her eyes. Away to their right was a high gray ridge of mountains speckled with the dazzling yellow of gorse in bloom. Immediately in front of them was a shallow valley, vividly green with young corn. In between the two a rocky hillside sloped up steeply to a crown of tawny stone fortifications.

Lydia gazed, fascinated. And then, as they got nearer, she saw suddenly that the whole citadel of Mycenae was alive and crawling, like an antheap, with tiny black figures.

"School day," shouted Marius over his shoulder, and at that moment a huge parking lot opened up to the left of the road with twenty enormous buses browsing like elephants at rest. Everywhere small boys and girls dressed in black smocks ran and shouted and ate apples.

"It's not how I'd imagined Mycenae," said Lydia mildly.

"Never mind," said Marius. "On the dot of twelve they all disappear like Cinderella's coach."

He parked the Vespa, and they passed through the gate in the wire fence and up the track toward the walls. They were already high up in the mountains here, and there was a feeling of great space and distance. The hillside fell away to their right, vivid green, running down to the low hills hiding the village and then to the broad plain of Argos, to the pink shimmer of Argos itself with the brown knob of its citadel on one side and so to the sea, misty now in the heat, a blur of gray-blue in the distance.

From below it had seemed that the fortifications were the highest point of the citadel, but now Lydia saw that the hill rose high above the line of its walls, steep and forbidding, dotted with ruined buildings that merged imperceptibly into outcrops of rock. And now the walls were before them, huge blocks of golden stone piled with apparent casualness, like a child's bricks—but so intricately balanced that they had stood for three thousand years. They were no higher that the walls of Tiryns, Lydia

realized, but she and Marius were approaching them from
below, and the stones seemed to lean away from them up
the side of the hill, giving an impression of strength and
grandeur and power quite different from the lowering
menace of Tiryns. And there, set back in the shadow between two enormous bastions, was the gate. Again Lydia
was reminded of a child's way of building. It was made of
three huge stones, one standing at each side and the third
flat along the top. But the childishness vanished as soon
as one looked at the guardian lions. They stood in a tri-
angle above the gate, one at each side of a short pillar, like
supporters on a coat of arms. The heads were missing, but
the tense bodies, with their curving tails and massive
paws, were beautiful. And highly sophisticated. Suddenly
Lydia remembered the cups and swords and masks in the
museum.

"Not lions at all, of course," said Marius in her ear.
"Lionesses. The female of the species. A very good idea if
you're out to terrify."

They picked their way through the crowds of children
and went in through the gateway. Below them to the right
was an enormous circular pit, edged with a fence of stone
slabs.

"The grave circle," said Marius. "Where your friend
Schliemann found all his stuff." He led the way down. It
was a sinister place, enclosed and airless. At half a dozen
places within the perimeter, the earth had been recently
disturbed, and three of the stone slabs around the edge
had been torn up and now lay flat on the ground.

Marius stood still and gazed at them.

"Well, I don't know," he said at last. "They can't have
been hoping to find anything—this must be the most carefully sifted bit of earth in the world. But *just* vandalism?
And they can't be said to have been very thorough. Well!"
He turned away briskly. "Now that we're here you'd better see the rest of it. Come on."

He helped Lydia out of the grave circle. Brushing aside
the children who swarmed around them like flies, they set
off up the hill on a steep ramp very like the one at Tiryns.
It was hot by now, and the hill above them looked enormous. Lydia faltered, but Marius kept up a brisk pace, and
as they climbed, the views on every side opened out.

Suddenly, far below them, a whistle sounded, and immediately all the dozens of swarming children turned and, like lemmings, hurled themselves down the hill, pouring in a continuous stream out of the ruins, through the lion gate, along the track and into the great buses. It took about ten minutes. Marius and Lydia stood and watched them go, and one after another the buses started up and moved majestically out of the parking area and down the road, disappearing finally around the corner of a low ridge. When at last they had all gone, leaving only a haze of dust along the road and a far, faint smell of gasoline, Lydia looked at her watch.

"At the third stroke," she said admiringly, "it will be eleven fifty-five precisely."

"That's right," said Marius, "and now it's ours." His voice sounded unnaturally loud. Lydia looked around. Far away below them a single black car was parked beside the Vespa, but except for the attendant at the gate, who had retired into the shade of his hut, there was no living being in sight beside themselves. The silence was complete. Lydia smiled slowly at Marius, feeling, illogically, that he had arranged this revelation especially for her. And all at once she was seized by an intense excitement, a feeling made up of the height and of the isolation, of the blueness of the air moving slowly around the high mass of the citadel above their heads, of the heat, of the smell of thyme—and of the silence, in which the sound of a footstep on stone or of a word spoken seemed not to carry at all but to bounce straight back to them from the close blue shell of air. Lydia's eyes dilated, and she shivered suddenly.

"I know," said Marius quietly. "I feel it every time I come here."

They turned and clambered on up the hill in silence. In among the stones and the grass were scarlet pimpernels and tiny yellow flowers like groundsel and occasionally a single anemone, vivid purple or crimson. It was hotter than ever.

"There," said Marius at last as they emerged onto a wide concrete platform. He padded forward quickly and disappeared behind the massive walls that marked the divisions of the palace. Lydia followed and found him standing in the middle of what had evidently been a vast hall, enclosed on one side by ruined walls and by the rocky hill that rose still farther above them, but open on the other to the blue air and the hillside falling away to the distant plain.

"That's what we came to see." Marius flung his arms wide.

They stood on the edge of the platform and looked down. To their left the hillside dropped abruptly into the gray ravine that separated the citadel from the mountains. To the right they could see immediately below them little squares and oblongs of stone wall in among the grass, and then, farther down, the great mass of the outer walls.

"Private houses," said Marius. "Built inside the walls for protection. But there are others"—he waved at the long green valley below them—"a whole village outside. You can't see much while the corn is high." He glanced vaguely over his shoulder. "Do you want to go on up to the top?"

"Is there anything one ought to see?" It was terribly hot.

"Not really. And the view is just as good from here."

They sat down and dangled their feet over the abyss. The silence pressed down. Lydia suddenly remembered Marius' flow of edifying information at Tiryns, but here he was letting her enjoy herself in her own way. She glanced at him gratefully and was disconcerted to find him looking straight back at her.

"*You*, now," he said without embarrassment. "Tell me about yourself. I know you came to a couple of my lectures, and I know that you're not after the Adelmann treasures, but there I really stop. Mrs. Erskine says you teach."

"That's right."

"And what do you teach? Latin and Greek?"

"All that sort of thing."

"And do you have a form, and do they come and tell you all their troubles?"

"Well, I have a form, but they don't seem to have any troubles."

Silently he considered the shimmering landscape.

"And in the holidays? What do you do then?"

"Stay at home. Read. Go for walks. Prepare next term's lessons."

"Or come to Greece?"

"Not usually. This is the first time . . . probably the last."

"I see. Well, I think you should do it more often. It suits you."

Lydia's eyebrows rose.

"I mean," he went on elaborately, "*it* suits *you*. As a background, I mean. Greece demands bone. And so few people have it." *Bone?* "Sideways, you know."

"Oh." *Good heavens. Whatever next?*

Laboriously Marius hitched himself along the stone and put an arm around behind Lydia's back. There was an immense pause.

"Is that Argos?" said Lydia at last in a strangled voice, pointing toward the sea. *A gentle kiss would be perfectly acceptable, it being so sunny and hot and all—but really, one can't wait forever.*

"What? Oh. Yes, yes, that's Argos."

There was a sudden splatter of falling stones behind them, and they both looked around hastily, Marius whisking away his arm as if he'd been bitten. A little man was balancing precariously on the hillside above them. He was wearing a dark suit, tightly buttoned, and his pointed leather shoes, slipping helplessly on the pebbly slope, were coated with dust. His face shone with sweat. As they turned, he averted his head and scrambled away up the slope, disappearing over the crest of the hill.

Marius looked after him thoughtfully. "Either Papandros is still keeping an eye on you," he said at last, "or someone else still has an interest. He didn't look like a policeman."

Lydia shook her head, overtaken again by anxiety.

"Well, *well*," concluded Marius briskly, turning back to her. He was clearly much relieved by the diversion.

"Should we go back?" said Lydia gently, trying hard to feel only amusement.

"Yes. Yes, I think we should. It's getting on."

They slid and scrambled down the steep path, through the great gate and out to the wire fence and the parking lot. The black car was still there, but there was no sign of the little man.

Lydia tied a scarf around her hair and climbed onto the back of the Vespa. Marius kicked it into life, and they were off, leaving a thin trail of dust to settle on the green corn beside the road. Lydia turned her head as they rounded the corner of the ridge and saw through the dust the great hill leaning away from them in the heat, topped by the golden walls. Then the ridge hid the hill from view, and almost at once they were through the village and out onto the main road.

The black car caught up with them at a level crossing, where a crowded, cheerful-looking local train was rattling across the road. Looking curiously into the car, examining the little man's motionless profile—he didn't turn his head, though it was clear that he was aware of them—Lydia waited for him to turn and look at her.

But the train rattled past, and the black car started abruptly and drew away from them down the curving road toward Argos, and the little man still hadn't turned his head.

"Marius, Marius, did you see?" Lydia was suddenly able to talk and move again.

"Yes. Yes, I did. I wonder. . . . Anyway," he shouted over his shoulder as they gained speed, "I'd rather he was ahead of us than behind!"

Afterward Lydia wondered why his words hadn't conveyed any warning, why they hadn't made her think more carefully. But as it was, she merely shouted back cheerfully, "Yes, indeed!" and settled down to enjoy herself. The hot air rushing past was heavy with dust, and the glare was tremendous, but simply to be chuffing along at high speed through a landscape half as old as time, perched behind Marius, leaning, in time with him, to right and left at the corners, feeling the sun hot on her face and arms, all combined in a sense of floating, timeless well-being. And when a vague rumbling, felt rather than heard, defined itself as Marius in song, she joined in contentedly. "South of the border, down Mexico way . . ."

They stopped singing out of deference to the siesta while they found their way through Argos, but when they were out again on the long straight road through the orange groves, Marius launched into something a bit more classy, and they were concentrating so closely on the tricky middle bits of Cherubino's song to the Countess that Lydia wasn't even conscious of the sound of another engine until the long black hood appeared at her shoulder. The car was keeping careful pace with the Vespa, inching forward, and it took only a glance at the deep ditch to the right of the road to realize what was coming. She saw

Marius' head turn sharply to look at the car, and in the next instant the black nose thrust toward them, the Vespa slewed violently to the right with a squeal of rubber, there was an appalling jolt, a slow, terrifying fall through thick dust, a brutal blow on the left shoulder, and she was rolling, somersaulting, her arms and legs tugging violently in different directions, each one crashing its own weight down again and again as she turned helplessly over and over. And then she was lying still with a great pressure in her head and the sound of the car getting fainter and fainter.

"Lydia! *Lydia!*" Marius' face was floating in some extraordinary way at the level of her feet. "Are you all right?"

"Oh, I'm fine." Her own voice sounded distant and unconcerned. But even as she spoke she realized suddenly that she was lying with her head at the bottom of the ditch and her legs pointing up the slope. Marius scrambled down beside her, swung her legs carefully down to the bottom of the ditch and sat her up. The pressure in her head subsided.

"Lydia, are you hurt? Where does it hurt? What—"

Lydia had a strong impression that she was the one who was keeping calm.

"I'm quite all right," she said soothingly. "Really, I'm perfectly okay. Honestly—what about you?"

"Oh, I'm okay. I didn't come off."

"Didn't come off?"

"No, the back of the scooter swung around when I braked—that's why you were thrown."

"You mean," said Lydia slowly, finding some difficulty in enunciating, "it didn't hit us?"

"Good heavens, no. We wouldn't be here now if it had. I braked to avoid it." There was an unmistakable note of pride in his voice.

Indignation flooded her. "But you might have *killed* me!" she said furiously and burst into stormy tears.

It was the large white handkerchief that reminded her of Henry James and the previous day.

"Always before lunch," she said apologetically, blowing her nose.

"Yes, yes, of course," said Marius soothingly. He had both arms around her rather tightly, and now he placed one hand, as if casually, on her forehead. Lydia giggled.

"It's all right," he murmured. "Everything's all right."

Lydia giggled even more. "I'm so sorry," she gasped, "it's just that I cried yesterday too."

"Yes, yes."

"I don't much usually. But now twice in two days."

"Of course, of course. Darling."

Lydia giggled even more. I'm so sorry," she gasped, breathing, so that when Marius started to kiss her with considerable concentration she had to fight him off almost at once.

"I'm so sorry," he said stiffly.

"No, no, it's just that I hadn't breathed." A new wave of giggles overtook her.

Marius gazed at her with some alarm. "Perhaps we should try to get back to Nauplia," he said.

Lydia was suddenly serious.

"Kiss me again first."

"If next term," said Marius after a time, his voice heavy with emotion, "I drove over to Cirencester one weekend, would you have dinner with me?"

Sound psaltery, strike drum . . .

Aloud she said, "Indeed I would. That would be lovely." She smiled at him.

Marius took her hand and helped her up the bank. Her shoulder was sore and her legs a bit wobbly, but otherwise, she decided, she felt okay. Marius dusted her off carefully.

"Marius, was he really trying to—to kill us, do you think?"

"I'm afraid one must assume so."

"Why?"

"So far," said Marius deliberately, "I have been unable to construct a satisfactory hypothesis."

The Vespa smelled of burned rubber, but it was still working, and they set off toward Nauplia at a dignified pace, Lydia clutching Marius with both hands and keeping her eyes tight shut.

The lunch party was in full swing by the time they got back. At least, it looked like a lunch party—Lydia never really found out how it had started. Two of the square tables on the Belle France terrace had been pushed together, and three of the waiters were swirling around with an altogether unusual degree of energy. At the head of the table sat Bubi, with Mrs. Erskine beside him, and Lydia was fascinated to observe that his arm was resting confidingly along the back of Mrs. Erskine's chair. Henry James waved enthusiastically.

"Lydia! I've kept a place for you. Here next to me." He pulled out a chair. "Waiter! Bring a chair for Mr. Blunt. What'll you drink?" One of the waiters hovered behind her shoulder.

"Oh, retsina, I think. Please." Lydia was bemused by the social atmosphere.

"No. Come on, Lydia. Try some ouzo." Who else had mentioned ouzo today?

"Okay," she said uncertainly.

"And what have you been up to? Mycenae this time? Goodness me, what energy, tell me all." So it was not until her ouzo arrived that Lydia was able to glance around and take in the rest of the table. And then she stared.

It was undoubtedly Mary-Lou sitting between Bubi and Marius, *but*—blue and white checked gingham with puff sleeves and frou-frou skirt, hair piled high and elaborate, bosom like two plump half-moons, defying gravity, above a broad ruffle of broderie anglaise, and face sparkling with smiles—she was barely recognizable.

"I think that's just the cutest thing I've ever heard," she was saying to Marius with gentle emphasis, laying a small brown hand on his sleeve and gazing up into his eyes. "You're just *marvelous*."

She pushed her chair back from the table and recrossed her legs in a dazzling flutter of white lace and brown thighs. Then she leaned forward again, her elbow on the table, and said simply, "Go on."

Lydia sat with suspended glass, her mouth open. But no one else at the table seemed even mildly surprised.

"How's the ouzo?" Henry asked. Lydia swallowed—and at once liquid fire consumed her gullet and poured down into her intestines. When the red mist cleared away and she had finished choking, she found that Bubi and Henry and Mrs. Erskine were all aflow with sympathy and advice—but not Marius, who hadn't so much as glanced in her direction. He was talking to Mary-Lou about archaeology, his voice deep and slow like a gramophone when the current is failing.

"Powerful stuff, ouzo," Henry was saying. "You've got to go easy, you know. Sip it. Try again."

Sipped, it tasted like aniseed and not particularly nice.

"And again. Got to get used to it."

Marius, reaching for his glass, brushed Lydia's hand. But he didn't even notice.

After a time one couldn't even taste the ouzo; perhaps after a time one wouldn't feel anything at all. That would certainly be an improvement.

"You were so nice last night, Lydia. I was awfully ashamed afterwards"—Henry raised his voice slightly so as to be heard above the steadily increasing volume of Marius on the subject of the walls at Mycenae—"inflicting all my worries on you and . . ."

Mary-Lou was clearly well used to making the most of unpromising conversational material. While Marius talked, she smiled shyly and cast down her eyes, she arched her neck and patted the back of her hair, she laid both slim arms on the table and looked at him sideways. Marius, plodding on, began to acquire the expression of a man who keeps on putting sixpences into a milk machine and keeps on getting out magnums of champagne. But when, finally, she responded to a sentence beginning "But leaving aside Eratosthenes' dating for the Trojan War . . ." with a burst of laughter and a wriggle of the shoulders that left her bosom all a-bounce, he faltered.

"Mr. Blunt is just *fascinating,*" Mary-Lou assured Bubi, leaning over toward him and trying to draw him into the happy circle of listeners. But Bubi, though he patted the hand that she laid on his arm, didn't turn around.

Mary-Lou turned back to Marius, sparkling. *"And?"*

"She is a lesson to us all," said Lydia ponderously, putting on her sunglasses.

"Yes, isn't she?" Henry lowered his voice. "So marvelous for her age."

Lydia thought about that for a bit, considering a large plate of rice that had appeared in front of her.

"But, Lydia, about last night—"

"Mrs. *Erskine?*" she said at last.

"What?"

"Marvelous for her age."

"Yes, of course, but . . ."

But Mary-Lou was marvelous for *her* age, too, come to think of it. Every day of nineteen and . . .

"Do listen. About last night . . ."

Lydia made an effort. Marius seemed to have found a second wind now and was leaning forward as he talked, gesturing freely. Last night, she remembered suddenly, she had thought that Henry was a murderer. That was hilarious.

"Ho, ho, Henry." She nudged him jovially. "Pure after all?"

It sounded distinctly odd, and Henry was flustered. "Lydia, dear, do please keep your voice down. *Please.*" He glanced nervously at Bubi.

"Okay," she agreed, chastened. "Shsh."

"Do you remember last night you said you thought you had heard of Eionai? Well, can you think at *all* where it could have been?" He had moved his chair very close now and was speaking urgently into her ear.

"Eionai? Well, it could have been anywhere. Homer, Aeschylus, Sappho—you pay your money and—"

"You know *Greek*, Lydia?"

"Certainly I know Greek, Henry. And I know Latin. And I know all about Greek history and about Roman history and about Greek verses and Latin verses. And what's the use of all that?" She paused dramatically. "I don't know about Life, Henry, that's the trouble. Strong on Greek, but weak on Life. There would always be time enough for Life, that's what I thought. And how wrong I was! It's never too early to start." She was really putting

it extraordinarily well, she reflected. "Even at nineteen."
She made a light insouciant gesture, and her glass emptied
itself onto the tablecloth.

"But, Lydia"—Henry mopped at the wine—"you should
have told me."

"About Life?"

"No, Lydia, do be sensible. About knowing Greek. I
need help terribly."

"Well, anything I can do, Henry. Just call on me." Why
should Mary-Lou *want* Marius anyway? He wasn't her
type at all, surely, unless of course she was simply tired of
getting no reaction out of Henry.

Mary-Lou giggled loudly at some rib-tickling sally of
Marius' about the middle Mycenaean dynasties. Well,
anyway, no matter *why* she wanted him. . . . A simple
hobby, really, requiring very little outlay or special equip-
ment. No knowledge of Greek or Latin required. Year
round, indoor or out, perfect for the kiddies—yes, that
was the bitterest blow. The kiddy. All those wasted years,
being educated, and now, on the shelf at twenty-seven,
while Mary-Lou. . . . Tears sprang into her eyes. How
terrible, terrible, life was.

"Look, Lydia, please." Furtively Henry produced a
much-folded sheet of paper and laid it on the table between them, leaning forward to shield it from Bubi. "Can
you read that?"

The words were written in ballpoint by someone un-
used to Greek characters.

"It's . . . it's Homer," said Lydia with an effort. " 'The
. . . elders were . . . in session on benches of polished
stone . . . in the sacred circle.' "

She paused.

"Is that really *all* it means?" asked Henry urgently.

But suddenly conversation had become general.

"On the yacht!" exclaimed Mrs. Erskine. "Oh, I think
that would be lovely."

"Do you like *boats*, Mr. Blunt?" Mary-Lou was making
sure that Marius would be coming.

"Miss Barnett"—Bubi's face was pink from sun and
wine—"please, you will give us the pleasure?"

A whole afternoon watching Marius watching Mary-
Lou . . .

"I'm so terribly sorry." Judging by her voice, she noticed with pride, she was desolated. "But I have a—hair appointment." What a fantastic excuse. But Bubi passed on without protest. "Mr. Blunt?" She was dispensable.

Idly she turned over the piece of paper in her hand. On the back were three more lines of Greek.

" 'Hoi d'Argos t'eikhon Tiryntha,' " she read aloud slowly.

"Oh, that's nothing," said Henry gloomily. "Just that list of names I told you about last night."

" 'They who held Argos, and Tiryns of the huge walls' —but this is Homer too." How like the Greeks to arrange a rendezvous for whiskey smuggling by means of quotations from Homer!

But the words had penetrated Marius' euphoria.

" 'They who held Argos,' " he repeated. "Ah, the catalog of the Greek ships! 'Hoi d'Argos.' " He flung back his head and beat time exuberantly with his arms. " 'Hoi d'Argos t'eikhon Tiryntha te teikhioëssan . . .' "

It went on for quite a time.

Bubi was all admiration. "But that is magnificent, Mr. Blunt! Please—please repeat, for us, that piece you have just said."

Marius beamed.

" 'Hoi d'Argos,' " he started again, giving it straight to Mary-Lou this time. Lydia noticed with pleasure that Mary-Lou wilted slightly, but Bubi was thrilled.

"Marvelous, marvelous!" he kept repeating.

" 'They who held Argos,' " declaimed Marius, in English this time, for Mary-Lou's benefit, " 'and Tiryns of the huge walls. Hermione and Asiné lying down the deep gulf. Troizen and Eionai, and Epidauros of the vineyards. They who held Aigina and Mases, sons of the Achaians, of these the leader was Diomedes of the great warcry.' Now you see" he started to explain with enthusiasm, "the position is that the Greek forces are massed on the shore outside the walls of Troy and . . ."

Bubi muttered something, rose to his feet and lumbered into the hotel. Marius didn't notice but kept on going, tipped back on his chair with his arms waving to right and left.

But Mary-Lou had turned herself off. There was simply no other word for it. She sat quite still now, her normal gloomy expression on her face, examining her cuticles.

Then, impatiently, she reached for her handbag and started to put on lipstick, entirely absorbed, as though she were alone.

Why? wondered Lydia. Tired of him? Suddenly had enough? She glanced around. Mrs. Erskine was smiling in a gentle stupor brought on by lunch and sun. Henry was deep in gloom. Marius was oblivious of them all—happily oblivious, so far, of Mary-Lou's defection.

Suddenly it was all *intolerable*. Furious, Lydia jumped to her feet, muttering excuses, and threaded her way through the tables toward the edge of the quay. Behind her she suddenly heard Mary-Lou's voice again, as animated as before.

"Hel-*lo!*" Mary-Lou made it sound as if Bubi had been gone three years. "I'm so *excited* about the yacht trip!" She was turned on again all right now, sparking on every possible cylinder, and all because Bubi had come back . . .

Oh, but how obvious! And how absurd not to have seen it before. Poor Marius. He had just happened to be in the line of fire. Bubi, as a target, certainly had more to offer Mary-Lou than he had. Poor Marius. . . . She skirted the edge of the terrace and plunged into the narrow streets behind the hotel. *Poor Marius* indeed! The hell with Marius—shuffling around, dithering and dathering —dinner *one night next term* for her, but falling off his chair with excitement the first moment some little blonde smiled at him. Beast, brute, prehistorian . . .

The heat was terrific. Dazzled, she stopped in a tiny square of white houses. An old woman in black sitting on a doorstep looked up at her with lizard eyes. A rich, fortunate young foreigner, that's what she was seeing . . .

All right, then, a truce to self-pity. Slowly she turned back again into the shade of the narrow streets. All right, then, so that was the end of Marius, the end of that particular little fantasy of donnish delight, of twin souls indissolubly united by a common interest in archaeology. Curtains for Blunt.

Familiar faces in a shop window stopped her again. Familiar, but here in this shuttered street, incongruous. Smiles, smiles, smiles—and that must be the Greek for "Only her hairdresser knows for sure." The new internationalism, the California girl next door presented as an ideal of beauty right across the globe. But would all those splendid dark-eyed, dark-haired Greek girls really prefer to have red-gold curly hair and china-blue eyes? Had the cult of the blonde spread even here?

Blonde—the very word was like a knell. She moved on quickly. But then, reluctantly, she went back to the window and peered at her own darkened reflection in the glass. Pale face, dark hair. And what did that add up to? Invisibility. Beside Mary-Lou, Marius simply hadn't seen her anymore. All right, then, if there was to be no self-pity, at least there must be action. Now. Now, quickly, before she had time to think.

The inside of the shop was familiar too—three basins and a row of dryers, faded pink walls, a pile of magazines, tasteful plastic flowers. *Home away from home*, thought Lydia, smiling nervously as the proprietor put down his newspaper and came forward across the deserted shop, voluble in welcome. He was plump and competent-looking, with hard brown hands. Lydia gestured. His eyebrows rose. *Really?* Lydia nodded vigorously. A long job, he indicated, pointing to his watch. Lydia nodded again. He shrugged. A small girl was summoned from the shadowy regions at the back of the shop, and Lydia, relieved of her bag and sunglasses and wrapped in a wide pink surplice, leaned her head back to the basin and surrendered, as to anesthetic.

It was indeed a long job. Lydia's neck ached, she couldn't understand any of the magazines, and as the afternoon wore on, she developed what was unmistakably and shamefully a full-blown hangover. "Tsigh-ee?" she said hopefully, remembering her success with the phrase book. But the little girl merely came back from the café next door with a tiny cup of gritty coffee. As her head started to throb, Lydia was invaded by remorse and fright, and when at long, long last the hairdresser released her from the basin and started to wind her hair onto enormous rollers she kept her eyes tightly shut for fear of what she would see in the mirror. He laughed delightedly at that, understanding perfectly, and patted her on the shoulder.

Under the dryer things were better. The warm air puffed and hummed, comforting, isolating her from all the world and even, almost, from the reckoning to come. Closing her eyes, she dozed.

When she opened them again, four other women had appeared in the shop. The proprietor was setting a massive blue-tinted matron, and two other women were reading magazines, waiting. A tall, bony woman was talking to the proprietor, gesturing energetically. It was Annie— Henry's *bête noire* and Bubi's "guide, companion and friend." Mary-Lou's so-called *dresser*. Cautiously, Lydia moved the hood of the dryer.

"What time?" Annie was asking—loudly, so as to pierce the language barrier. "What time?" She extended her wrist toward the proprietor, showing her watch. He glanced at a clock on the wall, shrugged and held up seven fingers.

"Seven o'clock? Not till *then?*" He shook his head. *"Really!* All right then." She was clearly annoyed. "Shampoo and set?" Vivid pantomine. He nodded patiently. "I'll be there." Annie turned away. Her eyes passed briefly over Lydia, anonymous under the dryer, and then she was gone.

Determined as ever, and yet somehow different. Lydia was puzzled. There was no reason on earth why Annie shouldn't be arranging to have her hair done, and yet Lydia felt a curious prickle of unease.

But now the proprietor, beaming, was bringing her out from under the dryer, the little girl had reappeared and was starting to take out the rollers, the other women had put down their magazines and were supplying an interested commentary—like the chorus in a Greek tragedy, thought Lydia nervously—and then suddenly her hair was released—but surely not *her* hair. Deep gold, corn-colored, it swung and caught the light. The proprietor picked up a great handful and spread it out above her head like a fan. Heavy masses shone on either side of her face. In the mirror her mouth opened slowly in absurd astonishment. The chorus exclaimed, the proprietor laughed out loud with satisfaction, and Lydia saw her own face dissolving into an enormous smile. She really did look absolutely smashing.

He was brushing it now, tugging her head back rhythmically, then coiling and pinning the long strands and smoothing around them a final, even swathe. Lydia stared, fascinated and unbelieving. When it came to leaving, everybody shook hands all around, and Lydia and the proprietor exchanged addresses like friends on board a liner.

"Ah, like the other lady," said the proprietor, examining what Lydia had written.

Lydia, saying a final good-bye to the small girl, nodded vaguely and stepped out into the street. It was nearly half past six now and quite dark. She walked slowly, without enthusiasm, back toward the Belle France. This was all going to be dreadfully awkward—a shamingly obvious gesture, it now seemed to her. Her motives would surely be clear to all the world—*including Marius*. Her stomach went cold. Why on earth couldn't she have been content with forgetting about him, thrusting him out of her mind, without—oh, for heaven's sake—bleaching him out of her hair? What an appalling thing to do, when a stiff upper lip would have been so much more to the point, so much more . . . English.

She stood still. "Like the other lady." *Like the other lady.* And it was *true.* Annie's voice, speaking to the hairdresser, had been clearly, unmistakably English. There had been no trace of the American accent—of the *assumed* American accent—that Lydia had heard yesterday in the restaurant when Annie spoke to Henry James or in the evening at the Xenia.

Suddenly she started to run, tripping and stumbling on the uneven streets, breathless, losing her way. So it was Annie—*Annie* who had come to fetch the Adelmann treasures and take them to New York. And Bubi, too, must be involved then, after all, and Henry, and Mary-Lou. She shot around the corner by the Belle France, expecting somehow to find Marius alone. But what she saw was Henry and Mary-Lou sitting silently in attitudes of exhaustion.

"Lydia?" Henry spoke doubtfully.

"*Say*—" Mary-Lou sounded for once really impressed. There was a short silence.

"Did you have a good time?" asked Lydia finally, sitting down at their table.

But Henry was only rallying his forces.

"But, Lydia, it's *marvelous!* You look *tremendous*—you really do, quite extraordinary—*honestly*, I had no *idea*—" He started to bounce. "But *why? Why?* I do think it's tremendous. I'd never have thought of it—"

"How *was* the afternoon?" insisted Lydia, to divert him. Mary-Lou groaned faintly.

"Not fun?" asked Lydia, delighted.

"Honestly, Lydia." Henry was reminded of a grievance. "Your friend Marius—"

"Not mine," said Lydia quickly.

"He made us all go Epi—" He groped. "Epidauros."

"Made you?"

"Well, he suggested it, and Bubi thought it was a marvelous idea, and so we all went and he made us walk for miles and miles, and he talked . . ." Words failed, and he closed his eyes briefly.

"*Why* Bubi wanted to go I can't imagine," he went on plaintively. "It's about the only place around here that's *not* on that bloody list. But there he was, charging around, looking at everything and that man"—he shook his head —"he never drew breath."

"Yeah," said Mary-Lou, summing up. "That Marius. He thinks he's the greatest thing since sliced bread."

"I can imagine," said Lydia happily.

But all the same she'd have to talk to him . . .

"Mrs. Erskine?" she asked.

"Lying down."

"And—and Marius?"

"He went off, thank heaven."

"Off?"

"Said he was going to Argos."

Was he *never* there when he was needed? She'd have to go straight to Papandros.

"Well," she began, "I think maybe I'll go for a little stroll."

"Yes, marvelous!" Henry was on his feet. "Let's."

"Oh, no, don't—don't you bother—"

"But I'd love to!"

"But—" She looked around.

"Go ahead," said Mary-Lou easily. She indicated her bare feet, elegantly disposed on a chair, and the dismembered sandals below it. "I'm through."

So a stroll alone with Henry it was. *This'll teach you to make I'll-show-you gestures,* she reflected bitterly, removing her hand from Henry's groping clutch.

"Like sunlight," he was saying wistfully.

"Oh, now, really, Henry. Please."

"No, you really are, Lydia. Beautiful."

He stood still to give added emphasis to his words, entirely blocking the narrow street in which they found themselves. A group of men at a café table beside them made loud noises of approval and encouragement.

"Oh, come on, Henry," said Lydia impatiently.

"Miss Barnett!" One of the dark-suited men at the café table had jumped to his feet. "Good evening. I am so delighted to see you." He clicked his heels, bowed briskly and, stepping forward, kissed her hand. "My—compliments."

There was a pause.

"Major Papandros," said Lydia reluctantly, "do you know Mr. James? Henry, this is Major Papandros—of the Nauplia police," she added nastily.

Henry's mouth opened slowly, and he backed away a couple of steps.

But now another figure was rising from the café table. Marius, his blue eyes circular with astonishment, came forward uncertainly.

"Lydia? Lydia?"

Conversation languished. Only Major Papandros was equal to the occasion.

"We must all surely drink a toast to Miss Barnett's new, er, *look*, don't you think? Not, perhaps, here, but shall we—" He indicated the street leading back toward the quays. "I have long admired your beautiful yacht, Mr. James," he began, taking Henry in a firm grip by the elbow and moving off briskly. "The lines are truly classic."

Henry, diminished and apprehensive, trailed beside him in silence. Lydia started off behind them, but Marius caught her arm.

"So this is why you slipped away after lunch without a word and didn't come with us to Epidauros!" His expression could only be described as arch.

Relief that he had failed to understand her motives wrestled with sheer, hard rage and left her speechless.

"I think I like it," he went on carefully. "It will take me a little time to get used to it, of course, but then"— he smiled conspiratorially—"I liked you very well before."

Rage won.

"When I want your opinion on my appearance, Marius, I shall ask for it," she said icily.

Marius blinked.

Oh, hell, thought Lydia, *how obvious can you get?* With effort she said lightly, "I'm sorry, Marius, but I'm —I've had rather a lot of comments on my hair. Inevitable, of course, but—"

"Miss Barnett! Mr. Blunt!" Papandros had paused at the corner of the street, still holding the unhappy Henry in a firm grip. "You are coming with us, I hope?"

"Yes, indeed! Coming!" shouted Marius.

"Now listen to me." He turned sharply back to Lydia, and she saw that his face had gone rather pink. "Just what the hell's going on? This morning you—you—everything was fine. And now this afternoon you go off, dye your hair and behave as if we'd never met before and I was being unpleasantly familiar. Now, why? Why on one moment and off the next?"

"Oh! That from *you!*"

They glared, and then there was a flicker in Marius' eyes.

"Oh," he said slowly, "I see . . ."

"Oh, come *on.*" Lydia was miserably aware that she had said far, far too much.

In silence they followed Papandros and Henry to the Belle France and found them talking to Mrs. Erskine. Mary-Lou had disappeared.

Mrs. Erskine now established herself finally with Lydia as a woman of sense. She gazed silently for a moment at Lydia's golden head, nodded once, said, "Very nice," and turned away to talk to Henry. Major Papandros, mercifully, followed her lead, and when the vermouths arrived he did no more than raise his glass politely to Lydia.

But it was not exactly a jolly party. Marius sulked, Lydia was miserable and abstracted, and though Papandros did his best to make conversation, there were plenty of gaps through which Lydia became aware of the intolerable Henry, protected now from Papandros and his sarcasm, getting back into his stride.

"I was never so surprised," he confided ringingly to Mrs. Erskine. "I mean, it was such a *surprise!* It's so unlike Lydia, isn't it? To do a thing like that. She's such a sensible person usually, I thought, and . . ."

Lydia, her head turned toward Marius and Papandros, felt her ears go red. Papandros was talking about wild flowers, and now she leaned forward to simulate interest. Suddenly she heard Mrs. Erskine say, quietly, but with emphasis, "You know, Mr. James, I have often noticed that people—perfectly nice, cultivated people—will give way to impulse once or twice in their lives, and behave in a way that seems very uncharacteristic of them. And this surprises all the people who know them, and it surprises the people themselves. But it's nearly always a good idea. We're supposed to regret acting from impulse, but in my experience that sort of action nearly always solves some problem that just couldn't have been solved any other way. It's not, of course, always the problem they set out to solve, but it's generally an even more important one."

She paused, and there was silence. Papandros must have stopped talking some time ago, and Marius was gazing at Mrs. Erskine like a man who has just seen the light.

But Henry James was irrepressible. "Oh, do you think so? And have you ever given way to impulse, Mrs. Erskine?"

"Well." She spoke meditatively, half to herself. "I suppose I married on impulse . . . the first time."

"Then there are the bushy plants," said Papandros loudly, "with flowers rather like your wild roses."

"Just four petals," agreed Lydia, making an effort.

"You will have noticed them in the hills, perhaps?"

"Pink and white." She glanced at Marius, but he was still lost in thought, useless.

". . . a little *cold*," Mrs. Erskine was saying. "I think perhaps I'll just go and fetch my jacket."

"Oh, let me," said Lydia gratefully, pushing back her chair. But Henry was before her.

"A pleasure!" he cried warmly. "No trouble!" He took Mrs. Erskine's key, listened carefully to her instructions and disappeared into the hotel.

Major Papandros glanced at his watch and started to murmur apologies.

"Mrs. Erskine, a great pleasure. You will excuse me?" He shook hands. "Miss Barnett, *au revoir*. Mr. Blunt."

He stood up and gestured to the waiter. At the same moment Henry appeared high above their heads on the wooden balcony that joined Lydia's and Mrs. Erskine's rooms. He was waving a fleecy white jacket and calling roguishly, "Shall I throw it down, Mrs. Erskine?"

What happened next seemed to take place in slow motion. The cheerful grin disappeared slowly from Henry's face and was replaced by an expression of mild surprise. He leaned over to the right, dropped, apparently, to one knee, and then, suddenly, as though the reel had sprung back to its normal speed, he crashed through the floor of the balcony with a tearing, splintering sound like the felling of some enormous tree and pitched head first onto the terrace about two yards away from their table. There he lay still, in an awkward heap, surrounded by broken timbers.

EIGHT

Of the spectators it was undoubtedly Mrs. Erskine who suffered the most. She exhibited all the classic symptoms of shock and had to be put to bed with hot water bottles and a drink of hot whiskey and lemon concocted by Lydia.

She hadn't needed the evidence of the cleanly sawed planks that Papandros extracted from the debris. "That wasn't an accident, that wasn't an accident," she repeated over and over again to Lydia when the police photographers had finished their work and the body had been taken away. "They were after me, that's what it was . . ."

Lydia wondered whether it would reassure Mrs. Erskine to be told about the little man and the black car that morning, since that incident at least suggested that it was Lydia rather than Mrs. Erskine that they were "after." But as Mrs. Erskine's teeth actually started to chatter about this time, she decided to concentrate on getting her to bed and to sleep, leaving explanations for the morning. Surreptitiously she ground up a couple of aspirins with the second whiskey, feeling like a poisoner, and had the dubious satisfaction of watching Mrs. Erskine drift almost at once into dignified but profound slumber, her exquisite head turned lightly to one side on the pillow. Then she retired to her own room, locked the door and settled down to contemplate the undoubted facts that some person or persons unknown had made two attempts that day to kill her; that it was now after ten o'clock and she had had no dinner; and, finally, that she had left the bottle of whiskey in Mrs. Erskine's room. The result of all these thoughts was a sort of chill emptiness—combined with a very definite desire to be safely back at home again in Cirencester. So when there was a furtive knock at the door and the mutter of a voice outside, she first considered keeping quiet in the hope that it would ultimately tire and go away. She then considered shouting out the window in the hope that one of the inscrutable, dark-suited gentlemen would come up and rescue her, and she finally considered jumping from the shattered balcony down onto the terrace. The one course of action that never occurred to her was to open the door.

So it took Marius, who, for reasons of his own, was not anxious to raise his voice, several long minutes to attract Lydia's attention and several more to persuade her that it was him, that he was entirely alone, and that he wanted to come in and talk to her. And as at first he ascribed her reluctance to open the door to her earlier fully justifiable anger with him, he was the more astonished when, after nearly five minutes of Pyramus and Thisbe stuff through the keyhole, Lydia flung open the door and drew him rapidly inside, clutching his sleeve and exclaiming, "Oh, Marius! Why ever didn't you say it was you?"

They sorted themselves out eventually, however, and Marius, who was perfectly capable of careful planning when the occasion demanded it, spread out on a spare bed—Lydia's room, too, contained three single beds—the large tin of pâté, the loaf of bread, the packet of butter, the bottle of red wine, the two knives, the can opener and the corkscrew that he had brought with him. No conversation was thus necessary or possible for quite a time, except that occasionally, as there was only one glass for the wine, one or the other was obliged to say politely, the hand already outstretched, "No, no, all right then, after you."

But even so the silence became, after a time, obtrusive. Lydia was consumed with embarrassment. Earlier in the day she had *finished forever* with Marius and had demonstrated the fact by provoking a blazing row, but now when he arrived she had made it all too clear how glad she was to see him. She glanced at him. They were installed at opposite ends of the bed, and Marius was leaning back against the headboard, his long legs stretched out in front of him, thoughtfully scraping out the last of the pâté and licking it off the knife. His ankles, brown and dusty between the espadrilles and the faded blue trousers, were sprinkled with pale hairs. Once either of them spoke, this safe pocket in time would be over . . .

But there was so much that must be said. She hadn't even told him about Annie at the hairdresser's this afternoon or—remembering suddenly, she put a hand up to her head.

"Take it down."

Lydia jumped. "What did you say?"

Marius cleared his throat and uncrossed his legs, knocking the canopener and the remains of the butter onto the floor.

"I said, 'Take your hair down.' "

"Oh. Oh, no, I don't think so."

She leaned over to retrieve the butter. "Marius, listen. This afternoon—"

"Don't talk so much and do as I say," Marius said loudly. He took off his watch and laid it tidily on the bedside table. Then he rolled up his sleeves. Lydia stared at him. Looking slightly uncomfortable, he sprang to his feet. "I have made up my mind," he announced. "I shall give way to impulse." Uncertainly, he loomed over her.

Lydia's end of the bed was heavily encumbered with the empty bottle, the glass and the dismembered loaf, and she herself was still holding the open packet of butter. Marius glanced around and was saved by his talent for categorization.

"We will regard this simply as the *eating* bed," he said firmly. "But now you—you come over here." He took the butter out of her hand and folded it neatly back into its packet.

"Marius, what on *earth* do you think you're up to?" said Lydia genially, sitting tight.

"Oh, don't *argue*," he said irritably, taking her hand and pulling her to her feet.

Lydia tried outrage. "Marius, *really!* For heaven's sake, do behave sensibly."

But Marius had put his arms around her and was stroking the back of her neck. With unexpected accuracy he drew out the pins, and her hair dropped heavily onto her shoulders.

"Ah," he murmured, burying his face in its folds and breathing deeply, *"the tangles of Nerissa's hair."*

"Neaera's," corrected Lydia automatically.

"Neaera's," agreed Marius equably.

He glanced briefly over her shoulder and started gently to push her in the direction of the other spare bed.

Lydia tried logic. "But why should *I,*" she asked, "give way to *your* impulse?"

Marius tightened his grip and bent her gently backward over the bed.

"No!" said Lydia loudly. Marius released her at once, and she sat down abruptly, illogically disappointed.

"I'm sorry," Marius said stiffly. He had his back to her now, peering cautiously out of the window. "It was just an idea. Perhaps another time. . . . Perhaps I should go?"

"Go?" Lydia spoke in spite of herself, the terrors of the earlier part of the evening flooding back.

"I shan't be far away." He turned around from the window. "In fact, I shall hang around quite near, I think. Our friends—whoever they are—seem to have been rather too active for comfort today."

Whoever they are . . .

"Oh, but, Marius, I keep trying to tell you. Listen. Tonight, in the hairdresser's, Annie—you know, that bony woman off the yacht—she was speaking English."

"English? Well, why not?"

"No, but I mean *English*—English English. With an English accent. Not American at all."

Marius stared at her.

"Are you absolutely sure?"

"Yes, I am. She didn't realize I was there."

"Well, I'm damned," he said slowly, at last. "Annie, traveling as companion to Mary-Lou. Oh, *hell.* I should have got that one." Savagely he kicked at one of the beds. "That means they're all in it—not Mary-Lou, of course, but Bubi and Henry and—"

Suddenly Lydia giggled. "I must say, it's rather nice to think of your taking them all to Epidauros this afternoon."

Marius looked sheepish. "You know, it really was the most extraordinary occasion. It was Bubi's idea, entirely, and then they all came—Annie and Bubi and Henry, and that appalling girl."

"Who?"

"That Mary what-not."

"Ah."

"In the most ludicrous shoes. And she and Henry *were* fairly uninterested, I thought. But I must say for Bubi—"

Marius paused and added doubtfully, "Whatever and whoever he is, he was really interested in it all. It's very rare, you know," he went on with enthusiasm. "A man like that, of not, I should say, much education, who is nevertheless fascinated by—well, by the concept of archaeology and the scientific study of the past, when he is brought into contact with it. When it's properly presented to him."

"Ye-es," said Lydia dubiously. Somehow, it didn't sound quite like Bubi.

"It was all so real to him. Now, for example, I showed him the tholos—the little round building with pillars, like the one at Delphi—and he kept asking, 'Is this where the elders would have sat?' and 'Would the benches have been polished?' and things like that. Don't you think that shows extraordinary vividness of imagination?"

Bells started to ring in Lydia's mind. "The elders," she said slowly, remembering with difficulty, "were in session on benches of polished stone in the sacred circle."

"*What* did you say?" Marius was startled.

Lydia repeated the lines with more confidence.

"*Who* said that?"

"Well, it's Homer—the *Iliad*, I think."

"Yes, I *know*, but who said it to *you*?"

"Henry—at lunchtime. He showed me a bit of paper."

"What else did he say? Or show you?" Marius' voice was grim.

"Well." Lydia concentrated. Her conversation with Henry in the hot sun had been so swallowed up by powerful events that it was almost impossible to retrieve it.

"Nothing else really. Only that bit out of the catalog of the Greek ships—the list of possible meeting places with Bubi's Greek contacts. *Oh!*" Lydia broke off, and her eyes widened.

" 'They who held Argos and Tiryns of the huge walls,' " recited Marius rapidly. " 'Hermione and Asiné lying down the deep gulf, Troizen and Eionai, and Epidauros of the vineyards—' "

"No, *not* Epidauros. Henry's list stopped at Eionai. Henry said this evening"—and Lydia grinned suddenly in spite of herself—"that he couldn't think why Bubi wanted to go to Epidauros, as it was practically the only place around here that *wasn't* on his list."

But Marius was not amused. "In other words," he said slowly, "I have provided the link they needed—Lydia, listen." He spoke with sudden urgency. "Bubi has a list of Greek place names. He doesn't know what it is, but he assumes that the place he is looking for is *on* the list. And he has another little bit of Greek that says that the elders are in session in the sacred circle on benches of polished stone. But none of the places on the list seems to have a sacred circle, or benches of polished stone—though he tries everything that could conceivably be considered sacred or circular—remember Argos? The dome of the church, and Mycenae? The grave circle? Well, anyway, then one day some silly ass—*me*, to be precise—quite gratuitously tells him that his list of names is from a list in the *Iliad* and that the *next name on the list is Epidauros* —and, what is more, this same silly ass then takes him to Epidauros and carefully points out the sacred circle— the tholos. Do you see?"

"Well, yes. But why on earth should Bubi—or Annie —be working from bits of Homer?"

"That must be Adelmann. It's just the sort of thing he would have done. Schliemann knew his Homer backwards, and I've no doubt Adelmann was the same. He must have been quite confident that if he quoted a well-known bit of the *Iliad* and stopped in the middle of a line, *anyone* reading it—his wife, or his son—would be able to complete it. He probably wasn't even trying to be mysterious. And he put in the bit about the polished benches simply so as to make it clear exactly *where* the stuff was. Epidauros is a big place—and I," he concluded somberly, "took them on a conducted tour of it."

"Well," said Lydia slowly, "so you did."

And suddenly, uproariously, they both laughed.

"Okay," said Marius at last, pulling himself together, "I must get hold of Papandros at once."

"But you know," said Lydia dubiously, "it was only— it was only this morning that he told us so firmly that Bubi and company were just smuggling. Are you going to wake him in the middle of the night to tell him that I've heard Annie talking with an English accent at the hairdresser's?" She had a sudden terrifying vision of Papandros' probable reaction.

Marius paused. "It's more than that," he said slowly,

but he didn't sound happy. "No, you're right," he said suddenly. "Even if I eventually got him to take me seriously it would only waste time. Much more valuable just to go and have a look."

"A look at what?"

"Epidauros." .

"*Now?*"

"They're bound to be there now they've got all the information."

"But, Marius, you *can't!* They've—I mean—Callos— and think of this morning."

"Lydia, dear, don't be absurd." Marius was clearly trying to be patient. "I only want to have a look and see if they've found the stuff. We know they can't get it out of the country. I can tell Papandros in the morning what I see, and then he can pull them all in."

"*Please* don't go. They'll kill you."

"Oh, nonsense, Lydia, don't exaggerate."

"All right, then." She started to pull some clothes out of her chest of drawers.

Marius stared. "What are you doing?"

"I'm far too scared to be left here by myself."

"You're not coming *too?*"

"That's the idea." She threw onto the bed green slacks, a pair of espadrilles and a thick white sweater.

"No," said Marius decisively.

Lydia opened her mouth to insist, but Marius was fingering the white sweater. "Something darker," he said.

She found a black turtleneck and put it and the slacks on. But then she looked helplessly at herself in the mirror. The gleaming masses of her hair—there seemed to be so much more of it now that it was fair—were floating over her shoulders and around her face. Twisting it rapidly into a big knot at the back of her head, she wound a long, dark-green scarf securely around her head. "Okay," she said. "I'm ready." Then, glancing around the room as Marius opened the door, she added, "You've forgotten your watch."

Marius grinned faintly as he picked it up. "I suppose you know," he said with sudden diffidence, "that I'd much *rather* we stayed here?"

Slowly he turned the watch over in his hand. "Here," he said at last. "You put it on. Keep you thinking of me."

Out in the open country, with the cool air blowing against her face, suddenly, unaccountably, Lydia started to enjoy herself.

For the next half hour or so they would be safe, just the two of them on the Vespa, buzzing along through the cloudy night. After that . . . She decided to close her mind to what would happen after that.

"A-hunting we will go," sang Marius cheerfully. He drove without lights, but the moon emerged fitfully from behind the clouds and then Lydia could make out the white of the dusty road, the dark line of the grass verges, and then, far away on either side, the dark shapes of the hills lifting themselves gradually higher and higher. After about forty minutes she realized that they were quite high up among the mountains, driving along a narrow, twisting valley.

Suddenly Marius slowed down and stopped in the shadow of a big tree hanging over the road. He turned off the engine and put the Vespa into the ditch, throwing over it large handfuls of grass and tall weedy plants that he pulled up from beside the road.

"Now, listen," he said. "The ruins at Epidauros are in two main areas. First of all we come to what they call the temple area. That's on the left of the road and covers altogether about ten acres, I should say. The tholos is slap in the middle of it. There's only its foundations left, of course—and that, incidentally, is true of the other temples too. So the temple area is basically an enormous grassy meadow with a series of stone foundations and a few low walls scattered about over it. That, as I say, is all on the left of the road, and there's a good solid wire mesh fence all around it, between it and the road. After that, the road runs into a belt of pine trees, and there's the hotel on the right. Then the road stops at a gate in the fence. Straight through that, in among the trees, you come to the museum and then to the theater.

"Now if *I* were wanting to have a good look around at night I would leave the hotel severely alone. For one thing, I think we can assume that they haven't got many chaps to spare and they'll need all they can use for the digging, particularly if it means shifting stone. But they'll be very exposed out there at the tholos, clearly visible from the road in daylight, so I should think, therefore, that they'll have somebody well down the road this way to stop any cars."

"How far away are we now?" asked Lydia, realizing uncomfortably that she had been thinking in terms of driving straight up to the site, glancing swiftly over the fence and driving rapidly home again to Nauplia.

"About a couple of miles, I should think."

"Won't they have heard our engine?"

"Possibly. But they won't be sure . . . I hope."

"So what's your—*thought?*" asked Lydia, trying to sound calm and practical.

"Well, ideally, we should skirt around to the left through open country from about this point, avoiding the road altogether . . ."

"But?" prompted Lydia.

"Well, as we don't know the country, I reckon that'd take us about three hours. Which we can't spare. So I think we'll just walk up the road and see what happens."

"You're joking!" exclaimed Lydia, agonizingly aware, even as she said it, that he wasn't.

"Now, calm down. They won't be expecting anyone, and above all they won't think that anyone on foot is likely to be dangerous."

"But we're *not* dangerous," said Lydia in a voice that squeaked. "That's just the trouble."

"Now listen to me . . ."

Two minutes later they set off. The narrow pass opened out almost at once, and from the shape of the luminous sky above them Lydia realized that they had emerged into a vast shallow valley, a saucer of dark hills full of fitful moonlight. There were no trees, but sturdy bushes spotted with tiny white flowers floated a thin, bitter-sweet perfume across the road.

Just four petals, remembered Lydia, *like your wild rose.*
If only she'd let Marius go and see Papandros she wouldn't
now be padding along in darkness and silence, terrified
at every step.

She was walking in the dust at the very edge of the road.
Twenty yards ahead she could make out the dark shape of
Marius padding along on the other side. There were occasional little rustles and quivers beside the road, and
twice she heard a dog barking, but otherwise there was
no sound except the patter of her own footsteps and, once
or twice, a scraping noise as Marius kicked a pebble or
trod on some stones.

I only hope he knows what he's doing, she thought dis-
loyally, wondering whether this peculiar order of march
really had any point to it or whether he had simply got
the idea out of a film about commandos. Commandos—
that was it, all right. Marius was playing soldiers and lov-
ing every minute of it, and she—she should never have
come.

After about twenty minutes she noticed Marius stop.
Cautiously, she drew level with him and then, in obedi-
ence to a gesture, slipped across the road.

"Look," he breathed. He was pointing ahead and to the
left of the road. About ten yards away she could just see a
narrow upright rod and then, as she peered, she saw that
it was one of the supports of the fence and that a continuous barrier of thick wire mesh about seven feet high
stretched away to their left. "We were nearer than I
thought." He spoke with his mouth right up against her
ear.

He gave an authoritative jerk of his head and set off
cautiously, at right angles to the road, following the line
of the fence across open country. The ground was grassy
but uneven, and they made a good deal more noise than
on the open road. From time to time Lydia peered cautiously into the thick darkness on the other side of the
fence, but for the most part she concentrated on putting
her feet down as softly as possible. After about ten minutes, a group of trees loomed out of the night, creating
suddenly an absolute darkness around them.

"Well, I just don't know." Marius leaned against a tree
and drew Lydia against him. "Nobody on the road, and
now, as far as I can see, no sign of life around the tholos.

But we can't be wrong about this. And unless they've got it all out and gone . . . We'd better go in," he said at last, dubiously. He groped his way forward and felt the fence. It was fairly tough but offered no footholds.

"You don't think . . . just go home?" said Lydia hopefully. Marius didn't answer. He took off his sweater and draped it over the top of the wire. Then, standing beside the fence, he bent down and clutched his ankles. "Come on," he muttered. "Get on my back."

The wire rocked and swayed, and the raw ends at the top cut into her hands through the sweater, but somehow she heaved herself over and dropped, noisily, on the other side. A moment later there was a crash as Marius, who had drawn back a few steps, hurled himself at the fence and managed to get both arms over the top. For a couple of minutes he hung on the wire like a spider, wriggling and groping, his legs waving helplessly, and then he had pulled himself over, the whole fence bending under his weight, and had dropped to the ground beside Lydia in a loud noise of ripping cotton.

"An old shirt, fortunately," he muttered, tucking the tattered remains into his jeans. "Anyway, we're *in*," and he set off back in the direction from which they had come.

He stayed close to the fence at first, moving with a caution that seemed to Lydia altogether exaggerated considering that their entry must have been clearly audible over a wide area. But she followed obediently, pausing when he did to listen to the silence around them, and placing her feet with care. They were in thick grass now and moved with very little noise.

After a while he struck away from the fence toward the center of the enclosure, and soon they were skirting massive foundations, great stone platforms standing five or six feet above the level of the meadow. Marius moved more and more slowly now, pausing constantly to crouch and peer and listen before moving forward again. Lydia, several yards behind him, was suddenly irritated by his caution. If there had really been anyone digging in this enclosure there would have been lights and movements and sounds clearly noticeable from far down the road, not this dark silence. They *must* be on the wrong track. Even as the thought occurred to her, she all but stepped on Marius lying flat on his front gazing down into darkness.

"Is this it?" she whispered, suddenly excited. "Is this where they've dug?"

"No," said Marius slowly. "This is the tholos, but it doesn't look as if they've been . . ."

Gradually in the starlight Lydia made out the lines of an enormous stone circle, enclosing a deep pit. Within the pit were concentric rings of stone, thick walls dividing the area like a target.

"What's all that?"

"Foundations. There used to be a dome on top, and two or three circles of columns. But that was in classical times. This is the really old part."

"What was it for?"

"Snakes."

"Snakes?"

He had taken a long step now and was balanced on one of the inner walls, still peering down into the darkness. Now he laughed softly.

"Not anymore. Not since worship of the Earth Mother stopped."

Lydia gave a sigh of relief and joined him on the inner wall. There was a scraping sound as Marius fiddled with a box of matches, and then a sudden dazzle of light. He held the match down into the pit. The stone walls were brown and damp, but there was no sign of digging in the beaten earth between them. He moved the match and looked down on the other side of the wall. At the very bottom a single crimson anemone flowered out of a crack in the stone, its stalk and leaves a vivid green. But there was nothing else to see.

The match burned Marius' fingers, and he dropped it, cursing softly.

"I don't understand," he said at last out of the darkness. "There's no doubt that this is what those quotations meant. The sacred circle at Epidauros. Nothing could be more sacred than this."

"Or more circular." Lydia spoke idly, not intending sarcasm, and was disconcerted to hear Marius catch his breath.

"I didn't mean—" she started apologetically, but he broke in, excitedly.

"You're right," he said. "You're right! Of course you're right."

She heard him stand up, jump to the outer edge of the pit and start off into the darkness. "Come on."

She followed him, jumping blindly. "Marius, please explain," she said plaintively, staggering slightly as she landed.

"As a prehistorian," said Marius discursively, moving away in the darkness, "I'm all too apt to overlook the lure of the classical period. I should have foreseen that Bubi would feel the fascination of the fourth century. Yes." He was clearly delighted with himself about something. "Yes." His voice was getting mellower. "Bubi, I would say, is by nature a classicist."

"Once and for all, Marius, will you or won't you tell me what you're talking about?"

He stopped at once. "I'm so terribly sorry." He came blundering back through the darkness, feeling around to find her. "I thought you'd seen it all and were telling me tactfully. . . . The theater, I'm afraid. Obvious. Plays were sacred ceremonies. And it's a true circle, of course, merely sawed off at one side where the stage is. And—oh, dear, oh, dear—polished stone benches. It's full of them. Enough for fourteen thousand people."

"The sacred circle. I see. And you think that—that Adelmann buried his things there?"

"Sure of it, now."

"But whereabouts? Isn't it enormous?"

"Vast. But"—Marius spoke slowly—"there's no doubt where. There's a single stone that is the center of the whole circle, the acoustic center. You know, the point from which you can be heard all over the theater, even up at the very back."

"I see, but do you think *Annie* will realize all that?"

There was an uncomfortable pause.

"You mean you *told* her?" asked Lydia at last, gently.

"Yes, I'm afraid I did."

"Well, anyway," said Lydia consolingly, without thinking it out, "that's were they'll be now."

"Yes," agreed Marius cheerfully, "that's right. That's where I was going." Lydia's heart sank. "Now listen. We'll go as we did before, with me a few yards ahead. There's a thick belt of trees up at the end of this field, between us and the theater. They'll certainly have someone keeping a watch up there, and we'll have to go carefully"—he was already moving off—"but as far as the trees we can move freely."

He was wrong. The man's arm encircled Lydia's throat before she had taken three steps. He was smaller than she was, but powerful, and he forced her head sharply backward and down before she could make a sound. Her chest and head filled as though to bursting, the pressure of the man's arm tightened, and then her feet, struggling in the long grass, went suddenly from under her and she fell back heavily. She felt the man go down under her, heard him gasp and heard, without understanding it, the stony crack. Then miraculously, the pressure of his arm on her throat ceased and she lay still, gasping.

"Lydia? Whatever are you doing?" Marius' voice came clearly out of the darkness, puzzled, but not particularly concerned. "Have you fallen over something?"

Marius, she tried to say, but it came out as only a croak.

"Lydia, is anything wrong?" Anxiety was creeping into his voice at last, and Lydia heard him moving back through the grass toward her. But then the ground beneath her heaved suddenly.

"Marius!" she said desperately, and in the same instant there was an explosion and a blinding flash from the ground beside her. She heard Marius shout, heard clumsy running footsteps, and the gun exploded twice more. In the echo of the shots there was still the sound of rapid movement, of footsteps scrambling and running, but fainter now, receding. And then there was the clear sound of a heavy body falling, a faint groan and silence.

"Oh, no," whispered Lydia. But the man had hauled her to her feet, had tied her hands together and with extreme urgency was thrusting her forward across the uneven ground, pushing her roughly or poking his gun painfully into her back if she paused.

"Marius!" shouted Lydia suddenly, but the man hit her hard across the back of her head, and she found she lacked the courage to shout again. But if Marius were lying there wounded, or even . . . . She stumbled along with appalling pain in her head and wrists where the man had tied her, but worse than that—*Marius, Marius, Marius . . .*

Suddenly she was aware that it had become colder, that the ground was smoother under her feet, and that the air was full of the smell of pines. This must be the belt of trees. Beyond it would be the museum and the theater. For the first time Lydia wondered where the man was taking her —and why. For he certainly had an aim.

The going was easier now, and the man pushed her roughly a couple of times to speed up the pace. Suddenly a building loomed out of the darkness ahead of them.

This must be the museum. The man quickened his pace still more, and Lydia found herself on a gravel surface, moving slightly uphill. There were no trees here, only a high lump of denser blackness right ahead of them. In front of it was a long, low shape, a building of some kind, with a diffused glow of light beyond it. They skirted the building, the glow of light becoming brighter every moment, and passed into a wide passage with high stone walls on either side. Three more steps and Lydia stopped abruptly.

They were in the theater. To her left was the dark line of the stage, and she found herself looking across a wide, paved space at the auditorium. The enormous semicircle of seats stretched upward into darkness segmented by flights of steps—a great, smooth, sweep of shadowy whiteness. But every line of the construction, every curve, drew the eye downward and fastened it on the vast circular space immediately in front of her. In the very center, tiny in the huge circle and unintentionally theatrical, a group of five figures was lighted by the powerful beam of a car's headlights.

The man thrust her forward again and called out loudly, and the five figures turned and gazed toward them. Three of them were men in working clothes—and the other two were Bubi and Annie. Bubi seemed puzzled for a moment, peering doubtfully into the darkness, but then, as Lydia and the man emerged from the shadows, he came forward quickly across the enormous stage, his arms held out wide in a gesture of welcome.

"Ah, Miss Barnett!" He waggled his great head at her gently. "This is a privilege. I am bound to say that I had not expected you."

The man beside her spoke rapidly, and Bubi replied. Greek. Of course. Glancing sideways, she recognized without surprise the little man who had been at Mycenae that morning. Bubi's voice was angry now, and he was gesticulating with energy. The little man replied sulkily, in monosyllables, and after a while he turned and disappeared back into the darkness. Bubi took her elbow courteously, ignoring her tied wrists, and led her forward to the silent group waiting for them in the glare of the headlights.

"No," he repeated. "I had not expected you. Or Mr. Blunt either. He was quite the best of the younger archaeologists in his field. I would say, and"—he shook suddenly with laughter—"an inspired teacher! Really, Miss Barnett, an outstanding teacher—"

"Welcome to Epidauros, Miss Barnett." It was unmistakably Annie's voice—but clear, amused and aggressively English. She was leaning back comfortably in a red canvas chair that had been set up beside the car. One hand, dangling over the arm of the chair, held a cigarette in an ivory holder. "Nice of you to come. I've been looking forward to a little chat for some time. The English abroad ought to stick together, I always say. And Mr. Blunt?" Her eyes slid around toward Bubi.

"Yes."

"But—not gone home early, surely?"

"*He* said"—Bubi jerked his head in the direction the little man had taken—"that he'd—" He gestured expressively. "I've told him to make sure."

Annie's eyebrows rose. "Okay, Bubi." She nodded dismissively and turned her attention back to Lydia. "So now there's just you—and us." Entirely at ease, one long leg crossed over the other, Annie looked at Lydia with gentle amusement. There could be no doubt now that Annie and La Gioconda were one and the same: her smile, which hardly varied, was the secret, inward-looking smile of archaic Greek sculpture, a gentle smile that tucks in the corners of the mouth and creases up the eyes but yet defies the spectator to share in its pleasure. Now she blew out a mouthful of smoke through her curving lips, and her eyes sparkled. "We shall have to find a use for you, Miss Barnett. I'm sure you'd like to be useful. Perhaps Bubi can think of something. Bubi's a great thinker— aren't you, Bubi? He thinks up all sorts of ripping capers, Miss Barnett. You'd be surprised." Annie struggling with

an ill-rehearsed American accent had been curt to the
point of eccentricity; released, she was enjoying herself.
It was Bubi now who was deferential and wary. "Perhaps
we could use your knowledge of ancient Greek again, Miss
Barnett. Such a bit of luck."

There was a shout from one of the workmen, and Annie glanced over her shoulder. "Coming. Right. Well,
for the moment you'd better just sit quietly. Where we
can see you."

She stood up and for a moment looked thoughtfully
into Lydia's face. Then her smile softened.

"Did he kiss you?" she asked suddenly. "Did that nice
Mr. Blunt actually kiss you—before he met with his accident?" She leaned her face forward, and Lydia, recoil-
ing, stepped back and found herself up against the hood
of the car. On either side of her the headlights streamed
into the darkness, and Annie's face, moving slowly forward again toward her own, was brilliantly illumined.

"Did he?" she insisted gently. "Did he? Was it here,
Miss Barnett?" The cigarette holder gestured lightly toward Lydia's right cheek. "Or was it somewhere . . .
here?" Delicately she drew the burning tip of her cigarette
down the line of Lydia's left cheek.

Lydia screamed. Throwing up her shackled hands in a
useless attempt at defense, she felt her feet pulled from
under her, and as she was flung down onto the stone her
head cracked back against the bumper of the car. Tears of
pain and fear sprang into her eyes and poured down her
face, blinding her.

Annie's voice said gently, "Don't do anything silly, will
you?" She turned away toward the workmen. Bubi followed.

After a time the pain receded enough for Lydia to look
around her and take notice. From where she sat, with the
headlights streaming forward over her head and with the
moon prevailing temporarily over the clouds, she could
see clearly what was going on. About ten yards away the
workmen, using iron crowbars and a heavy mallet, had
managed to lever up an enormous stone from the pavement. Now, as Bubi and Annie pressed forward, one of
the workmen took a spade and started to poke around in
the hole underneath. Looking up at the even sweep of the
auditorium beyond them, dazzling white where the head-

lights struck it, Lydia remembered her first impression
of the group as being in the very center of the open space.
As far as she could judge, the distance to the first row of
seats was roughly the same on every side. So Marius had
been right—the stone that they had lifted must be the
central stone of the whole theater, the natural center. The
acoustic center. Lydia stared at the rows of seats rising one
above the other, like enormous steps—hundreds of them,
it seemed. How could the human voice possibly reach to
the top of that? Even a shout must be inaudible at such a
distance. Shading her eyes with her joined arms she saw
that far up above her, beyond the final row of seats, the
hillside was thick with low bushes covered with blossom.
Wild roses? Surely not in such quantity. Mimosa? No.
Gorse—that's what it must be, just as on the hills above
Mycenae. By day the whole hillside must blaze with yellow.

The whole scene had become dreamlike now. The intent, grouped figures, the immensity of the theater, even
the pain—faded now to a dull ache—all added to the sense
of unreality. Even the thought of Marius was unreal. Once
she really took in what had happened, feelings still in
ambush would spring out and overwhelm her, but for
the moment she was numb. There was nothing she could
do but wait . . . and she was in any case so tired, so desperately tired . . .

"Look at that!" Bubi's voice, strident and triumphant.

She must have dozed, for they were all standing now
in a close group around Bubi, and he was holding up something that might be a sack or a leather bag, and he had
pulled something out of it, something quite small, that
gleamed in the car's headlights. A yellow gleam. Lydia
had seen that color before—in the museum at Athens.

"Look!" Bubi was like a child with a Christmas stock-
ing, pulling things out, admiring and then discarding them,
plunging in his hand for more. Yellow. Yellow gold that
tinkled like tin when Bubi dropped it onto the stone at
his feet.

"All right, Bubi. That'll do. Pick 'em all up now." Annie, relaxed but vigilant, gestured with her cigarette holder,
and Bubi bent down obediently.

So it was true—the whole incredible story was true.
Lydia realized suddenly that she had never really believed

that in this day and age there could be buried treasure—
X marks the spot. But it had happened. The map and the
code had been read, the treasure trove found, and now—
and now the story came sharply up to date. For now Annie would get her million dollars. But not until she got
the treasure to New York.

Lydia came fully awake. *How* were they going to get
these things out of Greece with every customs man in
the country watching for them? If she could just somehow
get away and get to the police. She glanced around her—
twenty yards to the first row of seats, then . . . her eye
rose up the endless rows, up to the very top. Not a hope.
They would get her even before she reached the first row.
Could she dodge around the back of the car, then, and get
to the museum and the hotel?

She glanced back at Bubi and Annie, immersed now in
discussion with each other. But they were less than ten
yards away—they would hear her the moment she moved.

"You're *sure?*" Annie's voice was audible for a moment.
"No customs, no passports?"

"Absolutely sure. It's part of Greece." Bubi's voice
dropped as he went on and Lydia heard only: "Roads. We
meet there," and again something about roads.

"Okay," Annie was nodding her agreement. "Okay,
Bubi."

Suddenly Lydia's stomach melted. Annie was looking
straight at her across Bubi's shoulder. "I'm so sorry you're
having difficulty hearing, Miss Barnett," she called out
pleasantly. "We have no secrets from you, you know. We
would only bother to have secrets if you were going to
have an opportunity to pass them on."

She drew gently on her cigarette, and in the same moment there was a movement in the corner of Lydia's eye,
over to the right. She looked around quickly into the darkness. The little man was standing silently just outside the
beam of the headlights. He looked awkward, reluctant.
Annie, following the direction of Lydia's eyes, peered at
him closely.

"*Well?*" she said. And all at once the little man made
up his mind. He stepped briskly forward into the beam
of light and started to speak, confidently and firmly. Bubi
asked a couple of questions, and each time the man nodded.

Finally he held out a man's wristwatch. Bubi took it.

"What was all that?"

"Blunt's dead," said Bubi, balancing the watch lightly in his hand. Then, smiling at Lydia, he tucked it into his pocket. "A great loss, Miss Barnett. The world of archaeology will not soon . . ."

Annie too turned to look at her, and for a moment her smile broadened.

Lydia sat up slowly, trying hard to keep her face expressionless. They were both watching with pleasure for her reaction . . . but—but *Marius' watch was around her own wrist.* For a second she caught the little man's eye, and at once he looked away. *Why* he was lying didn't matter, but lying he most certainly was . . . and so Marius had got away! Strength flowed back into her. *Everything was going to be all right.*

To hide her excitement she said the first thing that came into her head. "Anyway, you'll never get that stuff out of the country. The whole of Greece is looking for it."

"Oh, my goodness!" Bubi was delighted. "I suppose you imagine me saying, 'Nothing to declare,' as I go on board the yacht?"

"I'm simply telling you. You'll never make it."

"Get her out of the way of the car, Bubi." Annie, supervising the workmen as they lowered the stone back into its socket, called over her shoulder. "We'll want to turn it."

"The isles of Greece, Miss Barnett." Bubi giggled slightly. He continued to stand in front of her, taking no notice of Annie. *"The isles of Greece. . . .* There is more to the poem than that, I believe, and if Mr. Blunt were only here, no doubt he would recite the whole of it."

Something clicked in Lydia's mind. Not roads—*Rhodes.* An ancient city on one of the Greek islands . . . A meeting of some kind at Rhodes . . .

"Get her up," Annie's voice cracked, and Bubi sprang forward. He seized Lydia by the arm and hauled her to her feet. As, painfully, she straightened up, the scarf around her hair slipped off and her blond hair cascaded around her shoulders.

"What the hell—" Bubi stopped and stared at her. "Annie, look at this," he said slowly, and then, with increasing

excitement, he shouted. "Say, come here and let me talk
to you," and he beckoned Annie behind the car, out of
earshot.

Lydia, stiff and aching all over, speculating as they whispered, felt her new confidence begin to drain away. They
both knew, only too clearly, exactly what they were doing—and their plans would certainly not involve leaving
her to give the alarm . . .

She moved nervously and surveyed again the great
sweep of the auditorium. The bushes at the top closed in
the upward curve of stone. And then, as she looked, a single bush was caught by a breath of wind. A breath of wind
would be welcome down here, she thought. The night
was stifling . . . but—there *was* no wind! The air had
been absolutely still when they were exploring the tholos,
and even now—she looked sharply around the rim of the
auditorium—all the bushes were entirely still. Except
one . . . *except one.*

Her first reaction was one of pure happiness, her second
of acute fear—and, irrationally, anger. What could Marius
hope to do up there, beyond getting himself caught a second time? Had he already managed to get help? The police? But there hadn't been time for that. He was just taking needless risks when he could be doing something useful. There was not the slightest possibility of communica-
tion between them at such a distance. From where he was,
they must all look like puppets gesturing silently on a
brilliant stage, though if Marius were right about the
acoustics of the theater he would have been able to hear
virtually everything that was said when they were digging
up the center stone. But that would not include the word
Rhodes. Bubi had said that ten yards away from the center, over by the car. And that was the only word that mat-
tered . . . just that one word would give Marius and the
police enough of a lead to catch up with Annie and the
treasures before they were gone forever. *If it's the last
thing I do,* thought Lydia, and then, realizing suddenly
how literally true that would be, she knew she hadn't the
courage to do it. Annie and Bubi were still deep in their
discussion, but they would be bound to hear and . . .
just one word . . .

And then, up out of the depths of her memory, floated
a name—Tlepolemos. Tlepolemos, King of Rhodes . . .

he was mentioned in the *Iliad*. And Marius knew his Homer.

Quickly, then. *Now*. Taking a breath, she moved forward casually, as though to look at the place where the hole had been. The workmen were still standing beside the pile of tools, and they looked at her with interest as she approached. They were all three small and dark.

"Hello." She smiled at them nervously and looked down at the stone. They had replaced it faultlessly, shuffling dust and dirt into the cracks around the edge so that it was impossible to tell that the stone had ever been raised. Adelmann must have done just the same when he buried the bag. She pulled herself up sharply. She had to do it now if at all. *Now*.

"You certainly did a good job," she said clearly, facing the auditorium and raising her head. She glanced quickly at one of the workmen to show that she was addressing him, and then turned her head back. "Tlepolemos couldn't have done better."

"Signorina?" The man sounded puzzled, but not suspicious.

Risk it. "Tlepolemos—he's your man." She spoke even louder.

"Say that again, Miss Barnett." It was Annie's voice, just behind her shoulder. Her stomach contracted painfully.

Brazen it out. "Tlepolemos," she said firmly, turning and looking at her, "the man who originally excavated this theater. He—he was a professor of archaeology from Athens University, and he deduced from the literary evidence that there must be something of this kind somewhere round about here, so as a first step he applied to the Greek government for permission to dig, but . . ." She was into her stride now, prepared to pursue her mythical archaeologist step by step, but Annie saw her intention at once. Smiling, she pointed silently toward the car.

Lydia's feet pressed into the ground.

"Come along, Miss Barnett. I'm sure you would enjoy a short cruise with us on the yacht. You can tell us more about Tlepolemos on board—there'll be *some* time."

"You'll never get me onto that yacht." Remembering Papandros' words, *Every person going on board is checked*, she felt for a moment secure and defiant.

"Oh, you won't have to walk, Miss Barnett, just let yourself be carried."

And every parcel. "You won't get away with that either. The police will get—"

"Oh, no, Miss Barnett. The police will never get *me*. Come along."

"No."

"You are being obstinate, Miss Barnett." Annie's eyes flicked sideways, and she gave an almost imperceptible nod. "But I would advise you—"

The blow was not heavy, but it was expert, and as Lydia went down, it was into pain and deeper pain.

TEN

Lydia was back in her room at the Bourtzi—and she had the hangover to end all hangovers. The sound of the sea was louder than it had been before, and from time to time a wave slapped hollowly against the rocks, shooting needles of pain through her head. She rolled over and heard herself groan, but as much from the stiffness in her arms and shoulders as from the hammerblows in her head. She must have drunk far, far, far too much . . . and she must have mixed it quite abominably, because never, ever. . . . Where on earth could she have got such a head?

Ouzo.

The word arrived sharply from somewhere, bringing with it the lunch party on the terrace of the Belle France . . . Henry James . . . Bubi . . . Mary-Lou . . . *Marius* . . . and then, in a cascade of images, the whole of last night, down to that last moment in the glare of the headlights, looking at Annie, the blow from behind. Gingerly she put up a hand and felt her head. It was tender, not really painful, but it must have been quite a blow to leave her feeling as ill as this. Her cheek still throbbed where Annie had burned her.

She opened her eyes—and shut them again quickly, wincing from the glare of the sunlight pouring onto the floor by her bed. Then she lay quietly for a moment. At the Bourtzi the sun had just reached the end of her bed, coming from the window on her left. But now it was blazing onto the floor beside her on the *right*. Cautiously she opened her eyes again, peering under heavy lids. Straight ahead, about two feet away, was a small white washbasin with shiny taps and a mirror above it. A hospital. Of course.

At that moment one of the larger waves slapped against the rocks and her whole bed quivered slightly.

Rocks? Lydia sat up abruptly—and clutched at her head. She was in a narrow cabin paneled in pale wood with shiny chrome fittings everywhere. The carpet was soft and pink, and so were the blankets on her bunk. And then she glanced through the porthole above the bunk.

Half a mile away an enormous cliff of honey-colored rock rose straight out of the sea. On the very top, dwarfed by the scale of the drop below them, three narrow pillars of the same golden stone stood up into a hard blue sky, and behind them was the outline of low walls. For a moment Lydia forgot all about her immediate surroundings.

The sun dazzled up off the sea, and Lydia lay back and closed her eyes.

So she was on board the yacht after all, despite her brave words . . . and despite the customs . . . and presumably, since Annie had now shown herself able to get exactly what she wanted, this must be Rhodes. Her watch had stopped at five to twelve, but judging by the quality of the sunlight it was still quite early in the morning. The yacht couldn't possibly have made the crossing from Nauplia to Rhodes in four or five hours, so it must be the *next* day and she had been unconscious for well over twenty-four hours. She felt her skull again, this time with new respect. Had they got the treasures on board too? How could they possibly have managed it?

The door of the cabin opened abruptly to admit Annie carrying some brilliant orange and white materials draped carefully over her arm.

"How do you feel?" She laid a bony hand on Lydia's forehead.

It was too late to feign sleep, and Lydia contented herself with grunting and thrusting away the hand.

"Now listen to me." Annie leaned comfortably against the closed door. "You're going to do exactly what I tell you today, I can promise you that now. But there are two ways you can do it, Miss Barnett. You go on behaving as you are doing now—or you go along with us willingly. You choose. I don't mind in the very slightest."

"Okay," said Lydia and tried to make it sound meek. "I'll go along."

"I'm glad to hear it. Now get up and put these on." She was brisker and more businesslike than she had been at Epidauros, the smile less in evidence. Now she shook out

the materials and draped over a chair a pair of orange silk
trousers and a white shirt scattered with enormous black
blobs. They were just the sort of thing that Mary-Lou
would wear—they must, of course, *be* Mary-Lou's. Lydia
stared at them, and then at Annie, wishing that her head
were clearer. Annie's smile reappeared.

"Can't you guess? Not even when you've made it so
easy for us? All your own work." She flicked at a strand of
Lydia's hair. "The customs were very sympathetic. Young
girls drink too much, and then they're sick, and they pass
out and have to be carried home—or on board, in this
case—with their hair all over their face. He hardly glanced
at the passport." Annie's eyes sparkled.

Mary-Lou. So they had carried her on board with her
hair loose, showing Mary-Lou's passport, and in the dim
light the customs man hadn't seen the difference.

"Well, now, we're going to need a more active imper-
sonation today. You're coming on shore with us."

Lydia sat up slowly and immediately clutched at her
head again. "I'm not sure I can," she muttered.

Annie's lips tightened. "I was afraid of this—Bubi and
his hypodermic. You get up and I'll get you some coffee."

Painfully Lydia climbed down from the bunk and stood
holding onto the washbasin. She found she was still wearing her own underclothes, though her slacks and sweater
had disappeared. Slowly and with difficulty she started to
put on Mary-Lou's clothes. In a minute or two, she told
herself, when her head was clearer, she would grasp what
all this was about.

The shirt fitted, but the pants were tight and far too
short. Annie, returning with a large cup of coffee, looked
at her critically. "That'll have to do," she said, nodding.
"And don't worry about your face," she added as Lydia
peered into the mirror. "No one's going to see it."

She handed Lydia a pair of sunglasses and then, roughly,
pulled down onto her head a huge shapeless orange hat.
"Not bad," she said, standing back to look.

Lydia looked again into the mirror. This time she could
see nothing of her face except the tip of her nose, her
mouth and her chin—the rest was all hat and dark glasses.
Annie twitched some strands of Lydia's hair forward
under the hat so that they covered the weal on her cheek
and fell down over the front of the shirt.

"That's *good*," she said at last, standing back to admire the effect.

Lydia looked into the mirror again. No one who had ever set eyes on Mary-Lou would be deceived for two seconds in broad daylight. Who, then?

What Annie had in mind must be obvious—if only she could concentrate. Annie herself, it was clear, thought she would have guessed by now; her rapid sideways glances, as she moved about the cabin filling a large green beach bag with swimming things, were full of amusement and anticipation.

"Now be careful when you sit down in those trousers," Annie said at last. "Mary-Lou will be absolutely furious if she has to walk all the way down to the yacht with a great split all the way up the back."

Why should Annie care whether Mary-Lou was furious or not? The answer being, of course, that she didn't, but she was determined that Lydia should understand exactly what was going to happen. Lydia, it seemed, was going to walk all the way *up*—to where?— in these clothes. But it was Mary-Lou who would wear them to walk *down* again. So it was Mary-Lou whom they were to meet in Rhodes. And when they had met her, and she was walking all the way *down* to the yacht in her orange trousers, where would Lydia be? Annie's gentle smile dissipated any doubts that might have been left in Lydia's mind. *We would only bother to have secrets if you were going to have a chance to pass them on.* Lydia would remain on shore, no doubt, in no condition to pass on secrets.

Peering again into the mirror to hide her fear, Lydia clung to the thought of Marius. He and the police would have had more than twenty-four hours in which to get to Rhodes—*if* he had understood. But he *must* have understood! The police would probably be waiting for them on shore . . .

"Okay," she said, turning back to Annie, "when do we go?"

Annie frowned. "Very well, then. Now."

No customs, no passports. The words hadn't meant much when she heard them at Epidauros—she had been too intent on the rest of what Annie and Bubi were saying—but now they provided the clue to Mary-Lou's role.

If Rhodes was part of Greece, there would be no customs or passport checks on air flights between Athens and Rhodes. So the treasures were not on board but were being brought by air by Mary-Lou, who wouldn't need her passport to get into Rhodes and wouldn't have her baggage searched. But anyone leaving Rhodes on a yacht might well be asked to show his passport. And that must be why they were running the risk of taking Lydia on shore with them now: three people leave the yacht, three people—with the same passports—rejoin it.

"Ah, Miss Barnett, I hope you slept well?" Bubi, absurd in madras shorts, dark glasses and a panama hat. He waved authoritatively toward the rail, where a rope ladder hung over the side and dangled above a small motorboat. One of the yacht's crew was fiddling with the engine. Lydia, struggling with nausea, clambered down the ladder and sank thankfully onto the scarlet cushions. Bubi followed, and last of all came Annie, who had added to the inevitable seersucker housedress a severe straw hat, dark glasses and an enormous green and white striped beach bag that she carried over her shoulder.

The picture started to take shape. This was a beach party, a pleasure party . . .

Bubi gave an order, and the sailor started the engine and cast off from the yacht, turning the boat's bow in the direction of the shore. Bubi looked around appreciatively. He was confident and even jaunty again today, but Annie was silent and increasingly preoccupied. Her smile had disappeared altogether.

"A magnificent sight, Miss Barnett." Bubi was drawing her attention to a lateral view of the cliff and the columns. More were visible now—six altogether, joined at the top by flat blocks of stone. The boat was chugging gently away from the yacht, heading toward an enclosed sandy bay that curved back behind the cliff. In the distance, at the top of the hill above the bay, a small town of white flat-topped houses came slowly into view, but the country surrounding the bay itself was deserted. There were olive groves, a few fields and a lot of rough grass and rock. But except for a small white café on the beach itself there were no buildings at all.

Secure behind her dark glasses, Lydia watched the

shore eagerly as the boat moved closer. Where would Papandros have hidden his men? Behind one of the sand dunes? In the café? And Marius?

The boat was inside the bay now. The water was pale and warm, and the sandy floor was only a few feet below them, with the shadow of the boat flickering across it. The great golden cliff hung over the bay, and Lydia could see now that it was a huge circular tower of rock, a natural fortress strengthened with a ring of crenellated walls. the engine stopped, and the keel bumped gently onto the sand. The sailor jumped out and hauled the boat farther out of the water.

Looking to right and left along the beach, Lydia's confidence suddenly began to ebb. There was nobody in sight and nowhere that anyone might be hidden. And in the same moment a thought that had been lurking at the back of her mind sprang into focus: Rhodes had been a great city in antiquity, a busy port with a large harbor: but here there was nothing—not a ruined wall, even, not a broken column.

Bubi said, "Welcome to Lindos, Miss Barnett."

For a moment everything stopped.

"*Lindos?*" Lydia said at last, in spite of herself. "Not Rhodes?"

"This is the *island* of Rhodes, Miss Barnett." Bubi helped her down from the boat and maintained a friendly grip on her elbow as they started up the beach, "but not the main town of the island, which is itself also called Rhodes. All very confusing." He shook his head sadly. "But Lindos too is an ancient city, I believe . . ."

Even if Marius and the police had thought of the island as a whole rather than just of the port, how could they possibly watch the whole coastline? With helicopters? But in any case the chances were that they would simply assume, as she had done, that Rhodes meant the port.

"We will certainly visit the Acropolis later," Bubi was saying, waving a hand at the great rock above the bay. "And how we shall all miss Mr. Blunt and his knowledge of ancient history! This seems a good spot."

Bubi seemed suddenly to have taken charge of the party, and his voice was louder and more confident than usual. Now he gestured authoritatively at Annie, who hur-

ried up the beach to join them and spread out on the sand
an enormous white towel whimsically scattered with black
footprints. She also produced from the green beach bag a
chrome-plated cocktail shaker, three glasses and a camera.

Bubi sat down on the towel. "You sit here," he said to
Lydia, patting the ground just beside his legs.

"I should just like you to know," said Annie impressively, settling herself down at the other side of the towel,
"that Bubi is carrying a gun. Show it to her, Bubi."

With some difficulty Bubi extracted it from the pocket
of his shorts. It was quite small, lying comfortably on the
palm of Bubi's fat hand. But it was black and ugly and
convincing.

"So don't do anything silly."

It was out of character for Annie to belabor a point in
this way, and Lydia looked at her curiously. She was watching Bubi, who was fingering the gun with visible satisfaction.

"Okay?" Annie turned back to Lydia.

"Okay."

Silence settled on the party. Bubi lay back and tilted
his hat over his eyes, and the sailor curled up in the
shadow of the boat. Annie remained primly upright, her
hands folded in her lap, gazing out to sea.

Twenty minutes passed, and the heat was starting to become oppressive. Then, faintly, Lydia heard the sound of
an engine. A car was coming down the hill through the
olive plantations. A few minutes more, and she could see
it—a jeep, bumping down the rough track from the town.
It drew up in front of the café, and, incredulously, Lydia
saw that the driver and the man beside him were in uniform. Police. Lydia glanced quickly sideways, but still
neither Bubi nor Annie had moved.

One of the policemen was coming toward them now,
struggling across the sand in his high polished boots. Lydia
held her breath. But Annie was gazing calmly at the on-
coming policeman with an expression of mild interest and
curiosity.

The policeman was beside them now, standing at attention and saluting. He was very young and very smart.

"Good morning," he said in careful English.

Bubi sat up slowly, pushing back his hat and gazing upward in mild surprise. And suddenly Lydia realized that this was what he and Annie had been waiting for. This was the audience for their elaborate charade.

"You have passports, please?"

"Oh, sure, sure," said Bubi grandly. He waved a hand at Annie, who burrowed in the beach bag, throwing out two bathing suits, a paperback and a bottle of suntan lotion. Bubi had suddenly contrived to look extremely rich. Now he passed a hand affectionately around Lydia's orange haunches and gave a gentle pat. Modestly the policeman glanced in the opposite direction.

Annie found the passports and handed them over, shuffling forward across the towel on her knees.

"You are on shore just for one day?" asked the policeman, flicking expertly through the passports.

"That's right," said Bubi easily. "Just a little bathing."

"You will visit the Acropolis perhaps?"

"We certainly plan to." Bubi was contriving to sound bored—polite but bored.

Perhaps he would ask her to take the glasses off when he got to Mary-Lou's passport, or she could take them off herself. She put up a hand—and at once felt the pressure of Annie's shoulder against her own.

"Thank you."

But what was to prevent her standing up and walking straight over to him? Her heart thudded. *Now or . . .*

"Good enjoyment." The policeman handed back the passports, saluted and turned briskly away down the beach.

. . . never.

"Very good. Very good," said Bubi softly. He lay back again on the sand and replaced the hat over his eyes. There was a moment of absolute silence, and then he chuckled gently. "Very good," he repeated.

The policeman had looked at the sailor's papers and was struggling back up the beach. Lydia watched him climb into the jeep, saw it back and turn and then bump away up the hill, disappearing among the olive trees in a cloud of dust.

The charade was over. It had been highly professional.

"Well!" Annie was gathering up the bathing suits and the glasses and shoving them back into the beach bag. "What's the time?"

"Half past eleven."

"Another half hour and we can go." The roles had shifted again; Annie was back in command.

A couple of cars had arrived at the café, and a large family party was spilling down the beach, shouting to each other.

"Perhaps," Bubi suggested tentatively, "a little swimming?" Annie nodded. "But Miss Barnett," he went on, "or I should say, Marianne Louisa—will, I think, have to be *indisposed* today?"

"Yes—I don't think we'd get her into those trousers twice." Annie giggled, and suddenly both she and Bubi laughed uproariously. So the charade *had* imposed a strain . . .

Bubi, wiping tears of laughter from his eyes, took off his shorts and revealed a pair of iridescent bathing trunks clinging perilously around the lower slopes of his paunch. He walked with dignity down to the edge of the sea and then, after due consideration, advanced until the water was just above his knees. For a few minutes he stood still and admired the view.

Annie must have calculated that the yacht and her passengers were bound to be noticed by the police, but that if their passports aroused no interest at the start their best hope of escaping suspicion later lay in continuing to behave as much as possible like the superrich, yacht-owning tourists they appeared to be—tycoon, girlfriend and faithful retainer.

Now Bubi was lowering himself cautiously into a sitting position. Once there, he started to spoon water over his chest and shoulders with a cupped hand, puffing loudly.

A slight movement beside her made Lydia look around. Annie had taken the gun out of the pocket of Bubi's shorts and now held it lightly in her hand.

"Now *I* am carrying a gun," she said without expression. "The rest of what I said earlier still applies."

She dropped the gun into her pocket and turned to watch Bubi again. "Here," she said after a moment, picking up a towel. "Take this and go down to meet him . . . I'll be watching." She thrust the towel into Lydia's hands.

How much of all this was careful planning, how much inspired improvisation? From a distance, every detail must look authentic. Bubi splashed out of the water to meet her, jumping up and down and slapping his matted chest.

"Rub my back," he said quietly, still jumping. She couldn't bear to touch him. "Go on."

Lydia muffled her hands in the towel and dabbed tentatively.

"More." He was still jigging up and down.

She patted again, and suddenly he swung around, grabbed her by the waist and kissed her wetly on the mouth. She hit out at him, but he had ducked with agility and she barely touched him. Now he dodged away from her playfully, jumping up and down just out of range.

"Naughty, naughty!" he called out loudly. "Naughty, naughty!"

Lydia's stomach turned. She had played her part to perfection.

Annie strolled down the beach toward them. "That'll do," she said as soon as she was close enough. "Leave her alone." With a movement of her eyes she indicated the party of tourists, who were watching with interest.

Annie took the towel from Lydia and threw it over Bubi's shoulders. In silence they walked back up the beach. Bubi dried himself. As he put on the shorts, his hands felt at once into the pockets—and his face became tense and wary. He looked sharply at Annie, and she smiled back at him without speaking.

"When you're ready, Bubi," she said at last, "we'll go."

They set off up the hill in silence, first moving slowly and with difficulty across the soft sand but then more quickly along the track through the olives. Bubi led the way and Annie followed, holding Lydia by the wrist. After a quarter of an hour of steady climbing they found themselves on the outskirts of the village, in a small open square.

"Donkey? You want donkey?" shouted a handful of small boys, swarming toward them and indicating the high mass of the rock towering above the village. But Bubi took no notice and walked steadily across the square, pausing only once to take a photograph of the bay behind them. The other two followed, Annie with her arm now tucked affectionately through Lydia's. Bubi led them now into narrow winding streets between white houses. The street twisted several times, but Bubi didn't hesitate. He seemed to know exactly where he was going. And gradually the small boys offering donkeys lost heart and dropped away.

The houses thinned out, the street became steeper, and, looking sharply uphill along a narrow gray stone path, Lydia saw that they were on their way up to the Acropolis. *Mary-Lou will have to walk all the way down to the yacht.* Would she be up there already, waiting for them? Lydia looked at Annie, but Annie wouldn't meet her eye. She only tightened her grip on Lydia's wrist and slightly quickened her pace.

Far below them to the left were the bay and the sandy beach, with the boat from the yacht still drawn up on the shore. And above them towered the walls of the citadel. They were far higher than they had seemed from below and were built up as a continuation of the cliff face.

A high gateway led them to the foot of a flight of steep steps, and above that was an inner gateway. Bubi sighed but started upward without hesitation. Annie followed, moving effortlessly, always exactly six steps behind him. Her grip on Lydia's wrist was now hard and painful.

In the shade of the inner gateway was a table and a sleepy attendant. Bubi bought tickets, and Annie hustled Lydia through and out into the sunlight on the other side. The attendant didn't even look at them.

They were on the top of the rock here—a desolate, frightening area, vast and empty. Huge uneven plaques of rock jutted out of the ground, and the few buildings seemed dwarfed and pathetic beside them. In the distance, on the very crest of the rock, were the six columns that Lydia had seen from the yacht that morning. Below them, set into steeply slanting rock, was a great double row of classical columns with a fine flight of wide steps leading up to them. Nearer still—perhaps a hundred yards from the gate—was a square medieval chapel.

The high walls enclosed them entirely at first, but as they climbed, wide views started to open up all around them. On the landward side the village wrapped itself around the base of the rock, showing only the gray squares of its flat roofs. To the north was the sandy bay where they had landed, and to the south a curious lake, separated from the sea only by a line of gray rocks. And then, dwarfing everything else, there was the sea itself, curving right

around the base of the rock, intensely blue and hard.
There was nobody else at all in sight. They were as isolated,
Lydia realized suddenly, as though they were still on the
yacht.

Annie had hurried Lydia up the hill as far as the steps,
and now she shifted about impatiently, looking toward
the gate and looking around her at the rock and the walls
as though searching for something, still holding Lydia's
wrist in her hard grip. Bubi poked around in the chapel,
occasionally coming to the door to look anxiously toward
the gate or to consult his watch. The air was still, hot and
stifling. The sounds of the village came to them faintly,
as from a great distance.

Suddenly Annie stopped moving, and Lydia, following
the direction of her eyes, saw that she was looking at a
large circular hole in the stone pavement, more than two
feet across, with a narrow channel running down into it.

"Bubi! Come here," said Annie, relaxing her grip on
Lydia's arm.

"Hold her." She gave Lydia a little push toward him
and, dropping the beach bag, lay down and thrust her
head into the hole, peering into the darkness. There was
a vast cavity underneath.

"Fine." Annie stood up and looked hard at Bubi. Her
eyes were shining with excitement. "Well, for a start—"
She opened the beach bag, took out the passports and a
towel and put them on the ground beside her. Then with
a single gesture, she tipped the rest of the bag's contents
into the hole. They fell in a multicolored flutter. The cocktail shaker and the glasses tinkled softly far below them,
and then there was silence. Lydia looked down into the
hole and saw, with a sickening twist of fear, that they had
disappeared entirely, swallowed up in darkness.

"Very *neat*," said Bubi.

Annie smiled briefly, put the passports and the towel
back into the bag and slung the bag over her shoulder.
Then she took Lydia by the arm again and moved quickly
forward toward the chapel. The door stood open. It looked
very dark inside.

Suddenly Lydia planted her feet and hunched her
shoulders. Annie tugged at her arm.

"Oh, *come on!*" Annie's impatience erupted. She
tugged again and then reached out to seize Lydia's other

arm. Lydia started to fight in earnest, biting, kicking, shouting—trying to hold Annie off and at the same time hoping desperately to attract attention, to gain time . . .

Annie was taken by surprise and dropped back a couple of steps with her hands up to her face. Lydia went after her, but Bubi was lighter on his feet than he looked, and stronger. A blow on the side of the head stopped her, and in the same instant he seized her elbows and twisted her arms back painfully behind her. Then all at once they were through the dark doorway and into the smelly blackness of the chapel. Annie's voice pursued them.

"Now be careful." She sounded quite calm. "I don't want those clothes messed up. And be quick—she'll be here any minute."

Bubi hustled her into the far corner of the chapel where it was completely dark. He forced her down onto her knees, still twisting her arms behind her, and held her there. Any attempt at movement was agonizing, and after a moment Lydia stopped trying. They had it all worked out—the treasures would go into the beach bag, Mary-Lou would change into the orange slacks and the orange hat, and then she and Bubi and Annie would stroll back down the hill and go peacefully out to the yacht, observed, as their arrival had been observed, by the entire population of Lindos—and by the police. And Lydia would remain on the Acropolis, safely concealed with the cocktail shaker and the beach towel and the other contents of the beach bag, at the bottom of that black hole . . .

Lydia felt herself go limp, and she waited for the blow from behind her almost without fear. It was inevitable. Better to get it over.

"Bubi, come here." Annie's voice from outside the chapel was peremptory.

For a moment the interruption seemed almost unwelcome, but then, as Bubi dropped her arms and moved away to the door, relief flooded through Lydia, she crumpled, and for several moments she lay motionless, breathing the smell of the dusty floor. But gradually, when there was no sound of movement from outside, curiosity stirred. Shakily she got to her feet and moved toward the door, supporting herself against the wall. A few yards away, Annie and Bubi were standing side by side gazing intently down the hill toward the gate. There Lydia saw, without surprise, Mary-Lou picking her way across the uneven rocky surface of the Acropolis. She was wearing the briefest possible pink cotton shift and carrying a large, gaily colored straw basket such as one finds on every souvenir stall in Greece. So much was as expected.

But Mary-Lou was not alone.

A few yards behind her, choosing her footholds with considerable care but advancing steadily and resolutely, carrying a raincoat, a guidebook and the inevitable capacious leather handbag, came Mrs. Erskine.

Annie swore softly. "What the hell?" she murmured, and at that moment Mary-Lou raised a graceful arm in greeting, turning on her brightest smile for Bubi's benefit.

Lydia stared helplessly. If Mrs. Erskine knew that Mary-Lou was meeting Bubi here at Lindos, then surely Marius and the police knew too. But if she realized *who* Bubi and Annie were, why was she advancing so calmly toward them?

Mary-Lou's espadrilles made no noise, but Mrs. Erskine's sensible rubber soles squeaked rhythmically as she stepped from rock to rock in the expectant silence. *I must warn her,* thought Lydia wildly. *She doesn't understand.*

But at that moment Mrs. Erskine, raising her head, caught sight of Lydia standing in the chapel doorway, and her face blazed at once into unmistakable relief. She understood all right.

And now at last Bubi and Annie were both moving. Bubi had sprung forward toward Mary-Lou, ready to seize the basket. But Annie had dropped back a step, and as she called loudly, "Stop—that's far enough," Lydia saw that the gun in her hand was pointing at Mrs. Erskine. But Bubi too had obeyed the order, his hand still outstretched.

"I suppose you've brought your friends?" Annie went on as Mrs. Erskine halted.

"Why, no," said Mrs. Erskine with gentle surprise. "No, I'm all alone."

"My God!" Bubi's broad face suddenly registered the implications of Annie's question. "There's only one way off this place—" He glanced around him quickly, plainly remembering the terrifying drop on every side.

"That's *right.*" Annie gestured impatiently toward Mary-Lou, and Bubi sprang forward again to take the basket from her. Mary-Lou let it go without protest, gazing with obvious pleasure at the gun in Annie's hand.

"When do we start?" she asked with animation. "Where are the cameras? Will you be using me today? Why don't we—"

Bubi, running his hands anxiously over the outlines of the bag, didn't answer, but Annie said quietly, *"Shut up."* Mary-Lou blinked and was silent.

"Put it here." Annie gestured to the ground beside her. "And now you"—a jerk of the head to Mrs. Erskine—"over by that wall. And sit down."

Wheeling slowly to cover Mrs. Erskine's unhurried movements, Annie caught sight of Lydia, motionless in the chapel doorway. Her lips tightened. "You too, then. Against the wall. Not so close. Sit down. And now, come here." She pulled Mary-Lou a few yards down the slope and pushed her down onto a rock. "What do you mean by bringing her here? What happened?" She was keeping her voice down, but the words were clearly audible.

"Nothing happened." Mary-Lou was plaintive and astonished. "She was just there . . . at the airport. Athens."

"What did you tell her?"

"Nothing—she didn't ask nothing."

"You must have talked."

"Honey," Mrs. Erskine whispered to Lydia. It was hardly more than a breath. "Did they hurt you terribly?"

"No." Lydia kept her eyes on Annie. "No, I'm all right."

"No one. Honest," Mary-Lou repeated.

"You're lying, you little slut—I can tell."

Lydia murmured, "Did the police get my message? About Rhodes?"

"Huh." Mrs. Erskine's faint snort was unmistakably one of amusement. "Hundreds of them. All in the wrong place. They're at the port."

"Marius?"

"Yes, he's with them. Shouldn't be long now. I sent a message from the airport."

"But how did you—"

"Well, Marius told me Annie had found the treasures

and that he was following them. But then Mary-Lou . . . she was acting so oddly, paying her hotel bill and stuff. Usually she doesn't do a thing for herself."

Mary-Lou was starting to sound desperate. "I don't *know* how," she moaned. "I don't *know* how she got there, but she was just there. And all the taxis here were taken and . . ."

Mrs. Erskine went on softly. "The police didn't seem interested . . . so I just followed her."

"She offered me a ride, like I told you. And when I got here I couldn't stop her coming up here with me, could I? And what does it matter?"

"I see." Annie's gaze swung away from Mary-Lou and rested meditatively on Mrs. Erskine.

"Well," she said, "better not waste time. We may be too late already."

And as though to give point to her words, the figures of two young men appeared at this moment just inside the gate. They were too distant to be seen in detail, but there seemed to Lydia to be something faintly familiar about their appearance. *Chauffeurs?* she wondered as they started to advance up the hill, guidebooks conspicuously open. *Why do I think of them as chauffeurs?* And then, suddenly, she realized why: they had the same upright, almost military bearing that Callos had had, even in plain clothes. Policemen.

Policemen! And in the same moment Annie reached the same conclusion and, without hesitation, raising her arm at full length, fired two shots in the direction of the gate. The noise was appalling. But even as she shrank back against the wall and the two figures scrambled away down the rock, Lydia had time to register that Annie had made no real attempt to hit them. The shots had been no more than a warning. And as the echoes died away inside the rock, it dawned on Lydia that Annie must already have her plan of action fully worked out; otherwise she would never have done anything so foolhardy. Glancing around, she saw that Mrs. Erskine and Bubi had realized this too; they were both watching Annie with fierce concentration.

And Annie was enjoying herself. Her smile was back in place and her voice was very gentle.

"Well, now, Bubi." she said, settling herself down on a flat rock. "This is going to be a little job for you."

Bubi looked at her, and Lydia, seeing his expression, thought suddenly: *But he's terrified.*

"We tried something like this once before, remember?" Annie went on. "But this time I want it to work."

"No!"

"Yes," said Annie softly, as though setting him right on a question of fact. "Now, I want you to go down there and find whoever's in charge. Tell them I'll be coming out and I want to get to the yacht. Tell them that I shall be bringing one of these"—her head nodded toward Lydia and Mrs. Erskine, motionless against the wall—"maybe both. And I don't want any trouble. No trouble at all, tell them." The gun in her hand dipped momentarily as she shifted her grip. "And, Bubi"—her voice was very gentle now—"I do want to *see* you back. You can tell your friends down there, if they try to keep you, that if you're not back in half an hour I shall make a—a real mess of these two." Again her head nodded toward Lydia and Mrs. Erskine.

"Listen, Annie." Bubi squirmed inside his incongruous holiday clothes. "Why don't we both go down? You take one and I'll take the other. It's far better. They won't know we don't both have guns. And once we get to the boat . . ."

His voice died away, and still Annie said nothing.

"Look." He tried again. "I'll take a smaller cut . . ."

Annie threw back her head and laughed. "Oh, Bubi, you are such a—such a *booby!*" she said at last.

"No, listen—"

"Go on." The smile had disappeared altogether now.

Slowly, and with the utmost reluctance, Bubi started to edge off down the hill, his eyes fixed on Annie.

"They might shoot if I go alone." He paused.

"They won't. Go on."

There was a moment of silence and then—"Oh, now, Annie, come on." He was making a sudden last attempt at camaraderie. Smiling, he started to move back up the hill toward her. "You don't want to get all worked up like . . ."

Annie was not impressed. "Stop there." He halted. "Now turn around again and *go.*"

Bubi turned without further argument and started to pick his way down the hill.

"Well, ladies," said Annie pleasantly, looking at the three motionless figures and resting the gun conspicuously on her knee, "that seems to leave us a hen party."

Mary-Lou, watching Bubi's retreat with exasperation, threw herself down on a rock with her back to Annie and sighed elaborately. "You just don't ever let people alone, do you?" she inquired loudly. "You wouldn't ever want to let people *be*, I suppose?"

Annie glanced at her with amusement but said nothing. Mary-Lou shrugged and started to scratch with a long fingernail at a mark on her dress. From time to time she gave a heavy sigh. In the distance Bubi gave a last backward glance and disappeared through the gateway.

For a long time there was silence. At first Annie gazed fixedly at the point where Bubi had disappeared, but then, slowly but with evident pleasure, she turned her attention to the straw basket beside her on the rock. She prodded it, felt it, turned it around slowly, trying its weight—all with her left hand. With her right she continued to hold the gun ready on her knee. After a while she gave up touching the basket and just sat and looked at it thoughtfully.

Lydia too found herself gazing at it. It seemed enormous in the hot sun, bulging like some huge balloon, multicolored and shimmering, captive, bumping gently against the rock, the focus of all attention, the treasure, the reason, the justification. . . . Lydia blinked tiredly and tried to drive her mind to concentrate. She should surely be doing something instead of sitting here in this mindless daze of apprehension. She should surely make some attempt to escape, or—or what? As so often since the whole nightmare started, she had the sensation that everyone except herself knew what was going on, what was going to happen. And now this even included Mrs. Erskine, breathing so gently beside her in the silence. Why had Mrs. Erskine involved herself in all this? How much did she know?

Close to her ear Mrs. Erskine's breathing suddenly became faster. "How long will he be?" Her voice was loud and harsh.

Lydia jerked her eyes open, and Annie, startled, paused

with her hand on the clasp of the basket. "How should I know?" and then, with rising anger, "Why should *you* care?"

"I just wanted to know"—Mrs. Erskine spoke with sudden uncharacteristic vivacity—"how long I've got to go on sitting on this darn rock. I'm just so stiff." Laboriously she started to clamber to her feet.

"Stay there! Just you stay there!" Annie was in action at once, jumping to her feet, pointing the gun at arm's length.

Mrs. Erskine paused. "All right," she said mildly. "I'm only stretching."

But Annie was shouting now. *"Sit down!"* The gun in her outstretched hand shook and wavered.

Hysteria, thought Lydia automatically, and her stomach contracted as Annie started to advance toward them with the gun still thrust out.

"Okay, okay." Mrs. Erskine slipped down onto the ground again. "It's okay, Annie," she said soothingly. "It's all all right. All all right." She spoke gently, monotonously, and, slowly, Annie reacted. She stopped, blinked and gradually let her arm fall to her side. Then she turned abruptly and went back to her rock. She sat down in silence and gazed down at the gate.

Lydia found that she had been holding her breath and that her heart was racing uncomfortably. Beside her, Mrs. Erskine too let out a deep breath and slightly shifted her position. Mary-Lou, who had been watching the explosion with astonishment, sighed again and stretched herself out on her rock, tilting her face carefully to the sun.

Lydia shivered, and in the same moment Annie, astonishingly, gave an apologetic little laugh.

"You must blame that little attack of nerves on Bubi," she said conversationally. "I'm never altogether happy with foreigners, you know. Especially lower—lower-echelon ones. They don't have the same background as us, the same standards. Do you know Northumberland, Miss Barnett? It's fifty years behind the rest of England in many ways—fifty years to the good, I always say—you can still get real service there . . . or you could . . ." Her voice trailed away. "He's certainly taking his time." She frowned at her watch.

And if he doesn't come back? thought Lydia suddenly.

In his shoes, she thought, *I'd make a deal with the police.* And if he did. . . . *I'll make a real mess of these two.* She glanced sideways at Mrs. Erskine, and Annie, reading her thoughts, laughed.

"Oh, he'll be back," she said confidently. "You needn't worry about that. Because of these." She patted the straw basket at her side. "He wouldn't want to miss his chance with these. Cash on delivery, you know. He wouldn't be worried about you—nor would the police, come to that. But they're worried about these too. And they know that if Bubi didn't come back now they'd never see them again."

"I see," said Mrs. Erskine, and added conversationally, "You've got it all worked out, haven't you?"

"Yes, I have." There was a moment of silence, and then Annie's smile broadened. "And I'll tell you another thing I've got worked out too. I'm only going to need one of you to take down with me. Bubi's not going to need anyone. So you can toss for it if you like."

"And Mary-Lou?" said Lydia after a moment, but it was only a gesture of bravado.

"Mary-Lou? Oh, I don't think you can count her, do you? Not as a whole person."

But Mary-Lou wasn't listening. She had caught sight of Bubi returning.

"There," she said with satisfaction and started to smooth down her hair.

Bubi came bounding up the slope, a wide smile on his moon-shaped face.

Lydia, watching him, thought, *He's sold her out.*

"It's all okay, Annie," he called, stopping twenty yards below them to catch his breath. "It's all fixed."

Annie said nothing.

"Like you said," he elaborated, coming to a final halt just in front of her. "They'll let us both through. I told them we had two guns, and we'll each take one of them. The police won't interfere at all. We take them out to the yacht with us and put them into a boat as we leave territorial waters. The police'll pick them up." He was very excited.

The police must have had that plan all ready, thought Lydia. Which bit isn't true?

"Well, well," said Annie gently. "That's good, Bubi.

Not quite what I said, in fact, but good. Very good." But she didn't look pleased, and Bubi, watching her, started to lose his ebullience.

"It's all arranged," he repeated anxiously. "Like you said."

"Do you know, Bubi," Annie said thoughtfully, her lips drawn back gently into their habitual smile. "I don't altogether believe you."

Turning her head to glance at Mrs. Erskine, Lydia missed the slight movement of Annie's right hand and the shot brought her heart into her mouth. She was just in time to see Bubi throw himself violently to the ground, and she reflected with wry admiration that Annie was certainly doing her best to scare the daylights out of him.

Then, deliberately, Annie fired twice more into the dying body, and Mrs. Erskine said loudly, "She's mad." But it was Mary-Lou who acted. For her, Bubi's death meant, pure and simply, the end of her career in films.

"She shot him," she said with slow amazement. "She shot him." And then she turned on Annie a face unrecognizable with fury. "I believe you're *jealous!*" In the next second she had leaped to her feet and flung herself at Annie, scratching, kicking and biting.

Annie was taken by surprise. Under the shock of the attack she fell awkwardly sideways, dropping the gun, and started to defend herself with her hands. But she recovered quickly, and it took her only a few seconds to throw Mary-Lou off, to seize her wrists and wrench her arms behind her. Huddled on the ground, her face crushed into the rock, Mary-Lou screamed with pain.

Lydia had sat motionless, but now, in the brief moment in which Annie, kneeling on Mary-Lou's back, glanced around her for the gun, she found herself suddenly on her feet. She flung herself forward at full length, knocking the gun aside just as Annie's hand touched it. Skidding across the tilted surface of the rock, it fell with a metallic clatter into a narrow crack, and in a second Annie was after it, reaching her long arm down, groping along the crevice. Lydia, prone and breathless on the rock, became aware suddenly of shouts and a crackle of gunfire from the direction of the gate. Raising her head like a startled animal, Annie glanced quickly down the hill and plunged her arm again into the crack. But the shouts increased in volume. Lydia could hear running footsteps—the rasp of nailed boots on rock—and Annie, glancing around once again, jumped to her feet, grabbed the straw basket and ran off up the hill with long athletic strides.

Footsteps and excited voices went rapidly past Lydia, and then a pair of highly polished boots strode across her line of vision and a familiar voice said courteously, "That was excellent, Miss Barnett. Excellent." The next moment she heard him stop beside Mrs. Erskine and say, "Ah, madame, I am so glad to see you safe. You have suffered no—inconvenience—I hope?"

How like Papandros, thought Lydia bitterly, to ignore *her* danger and "inconvenience." With a groan, less of pain than of shame at her own pettiness, she rolled over onto her back and sat up.

Annie had reached the great flight of steps and was starting up them. As she made the top, she glanced back at the three young policemen, now gaining on her, and put on a further burst of speed.

"Lydia." Marius was crouching on the rock beside her. As she turned to him eagerly, his eyes went at once to the angry weal on her cheek. "Did Annie do that?"

"What? Yes, but, oh *Marius* . . ."

But he had already gone, loping up the hill with enormous steps.

Papandros cupped his hands and roared something after him in Greek.

"I am saying," he explained to Mrs. Erskine, "that they need not hurry. There is no way off the rock up there, and we are bound to apprehend her."

"But—" Mesmerized for a moment by Papandros' certainty and by Marius' abrupt arrival and departure, Lydia gazed at the running figures on the skyline. Marius had paused for a moment and nodded, but now he had gone on again. It was true that beyond the columns at the peak of the rock there was nothing but the vast terrifying drop to the sea, and yet—Annie was heading that way with absolute determination, as though she knew exactly where she was going. For a moment, fantastic visions of Annie leaping from the rock and being picked up from the sea by a boat from the yacht flashed through Lydia's head, and then, suddenly, as another thought struck her, she herself was running desperately up the hill in pursuit.

"The *treasures!*" she shouted over her shoulder as she went. Neither Papandros nor Marius, she had realized suddenly, had any idea what was in Annie's basket. Annie was once again holding them all to ransom, threatening to throw the treasures off the rock, bartering their safety for her own, getting away after all, even now, at the eleventh hour . . .

At every moment Lydia expected to hear Papandros' footsteps behind her, but when she paused for breath at the foot of the steps, he was still standing tranquilly beside Mrs. Erskine. So he hadn't understood, even now. Or perhaps he hadn't heard. Taking a deep breath, she started up the steps.

And as she reached the top, she saw that her guess had been right. Annie was standing against the sky at the very edge of the rock, shouting at the three policemen who, warily now, were closing in on her. Marius was still some distance away but moving very fast.

"Don't you come any closer!" Annie shouted, and Lydia could see that her whole body was shaking. "Don't you dare! I'll—" She swung the basket expressively.

But the policemen, half crouching now, took no notice. Marius had caught up with them, and all four were moving forward with the greatest caution, on the very edge of the cliff. Lydia, gasping for breath, shouted, "Marius! Stop!" but her voice was barely audible.

"Stop!" screamed Annie in the same moment, and when again the men took no notice, she swung the basket in a wide arc and then—deliberately or not Lydia could never be sure—let go. The basket curved up into the blue air and—slowly, slowly—dipped below the line of the rock and disappeared.

Lydia sat down abruptly. Annie was still standing at the edge of the rock, and the four men, undeterred, were still advancing cautiously. But the contest, thought Lydia, was over. Even though she would certainly now be captured, Annie had made sure that the treasures were lost forever.

And then—so suddenly that Marius and the policemen were left in their cautious, half-crouching attitudes; so silently that Lydia blinked, wondering if she had really seen it happen—Annie turned, took two steps and disappeared over the edge of the rock.

Looking down from that height made Lydia feel dizzy. And in any case there was nothing to see except the distant barely rippled surface of the Mediterranean. Even the foot of the cliff on which they were standing was hidden, so steep was the drop.

A hand grasped Lydia's arm and drew her away from the edge. One of the young policemen offered her a cigarette, and she waited patiently while he attempted with shaking hands to light a match. When at last the cigarette was lighted, she remembered without surprise that she didn't smoke, and tossed it away over her shoulder. The little cylinder somersaulted and disappeared over the edge of the cliff, and Lydia, to her own astonishment, found herself weeping painfully.

"Perhaps better that way, you know. She must have been quite mad."

Marius sounded calm, detached—almost patronizing.

Lydia felt a sudden spurt of anger. "Don't you care?" she asked. "Even about the treasures?"

"I'm more concerned, actually, about you."

"Oh, I'm okay . . . but that could have been prevented."

"Don't worry about Annie."

"I'm not! But the treasures—they needn't have been lost."

"Never mind," Marius said gently. "Let's go down."

He took her arm, but she snatched it away. "I *do* mind," she said childishly.

But there was no point in staying where they were. The policemen had long since disappeared, and the emptiness of the sky and the rock were horrible. Lydia wiped her eyes and blew her nose. In uncomfortable silence they started back down the hill.

As they reached the top of the great flight of steps, they both stopped and looked back. The columns stood up, honey-colored, against the sky—just as Lydia had first seen them from the yacht, early that morning.

"Give me time," Lydia said, though Marius had said nothing.

"All the time in the world," he replied seriously, and they went on down together.

Papandros and Mrs Erskine were standing side by side like a reception committee, and Lydia had the impression that neither of them had spoken or moved since she dashed away from them up the hill. But the body had been removed, and Mary-Lou was nowhere to be seen, so Papandros must in fact have made decisions and given orders.

"Hi, honey," said Mrs. Erskine, but she too seemed drained of emotion.

There was nothing more to be said.

"Could we go?" said Lydia at last, and at once Mrs. Erskine turned eagerly toward the gate.

But Papandros didn't follow them, and after a moment they felt obliged to stop and look back at him.

"You know," he said loudly, "the treasures mean a great deal to Greece. They are part of her heritage, a very precious part."

Lydia stared at him in astonishment.

"I would make—" He corrected himself. "The police would make *great* concessions to secure them . . ."

For heaven's sake, thought Lydia, overcome again with tiredness. *Is this some kind of apology for not having taken me seriously?*

Aloud she said rudely, "You're too late."

Papandros took no notice. "There would, for example," he said, "be no prosecution if I could secure them. Today."

With a burst of irritation Lydia turned away and, taking Mrs. Erskine's elbow in a firm grip, started off again down the hill. Marius followed them, and so, after a time, did Papandros.

It seemed a long way down to the gate. The going was rough. The sun was at its hottest, and Lydia was begining to long for shade and something cold to drink, but Mrs. Erskine, far from hurrying, began to go slower and slower. Finally, just as they reached the gatehouse, she detached herself gently from Lydia's grasp and stopped altogether. Behind them Papandros and Marius stopped too.

Mrs. Erskine sighed and shifted her raincoat and heavy bag to the other hand. She turned round to face the two men.

"The Heritage of Greece," she said sadly, and once again the capital letters were clearly indicated.

Papandros took a step forward.

"Just let me get my compact out," she said at last. "I'll bet my nose is shining."

Opening her enormous bag, she extracted from it a compact and then, with a tiny rueful smile, handed the bag to Papandros. And he, almost incredulous, speechless from excitement and relief, sat down abruptly on the ground and started to take out of it cups and crowns and daggers and brooches, all dented and worn—but all gleaming with the unmistakable yellow gleam of gold.

"Honey, please say you're not too mad at me."

Explanations—inevitable and imminent—had been hovering in the air for some time, but this was far from the beginning that Lydia had expected. It had now been half an hour since they had finally left the citadel, ten minutes since Papandros and his crew-cut supporters had driven off towards Rhodes and Athens, taking with them a protesting Mary-Lou. Since that moment, none of the remaining three had said a word, except when Marius, steering Lydia and Mrs. Erskine into a small deserted café, had announced loudly to the waiter, "I want a bottle of white vermouth, a gallon of soda and three glasses."

Now, as Lydia gazed at her in astonishment, Mrs. Erskine, mistaking her expression, went on earnestly. "You see, dear, it was really only thoughtlessness. I didn't realize till that night when poor Mr. James was killed that I was putting you in danger. Poor Mr. Callos, of course . . . but at that time I still wasn't quite sure. But when it might have been *you* who got hurt, I saw that things had gone quite far enough. I felt just terrible. So as soon as I woke up, I went right out and I found Major Papandros and—and I told him."

She stopped and leaned back, confident of having explained everything.

"Told him what?" said Lydia at last.

"Why—who the treasures belonged to, of course."

"But they belong to the Greek government."

"No, dear," said Mrs. Erskine quietly. "They belong to me."

Marius, who had been shifting uncomfortably in his chair, intervened swiftly. "Mrs. Erskine," he said, "is Gustav Adelmann's widow."

"Gustav? The son? Oh, *no!* So your name isn't Erskine at all?"

"Of course it is, dear! I was only married to Gustav for a few months, when I was just a girl—barely seventeen. He was *very* handsome," she added, as though the point needed clearing up. "And so I knew all about the treasures. Gustav was always talking about them and how we'd go and find them one day, when his mother died. But instead, he died himself . . . And after that I married Mr. Erskine. So I was downright furious when they stole those letters and things last month, and I decided just to come and see what was going on. I reckoned I had a right to be here."

Lydia turned slowly to Marius. "And you knew all this all the time?"

"I only suspected."

"And Bubi and Annie? Did they know too?"

"Oh, yes, dear, they must have known," said Mrs. Erskine. "That's why they were trying so hard to—to dispose of me. You see. Rigging the balcony to collapse, and—"

"And I thought it was me," said Lydia slowly. "But—but what about when they tried to kill *us*—Marius and me, on the Vespa? On the way back from Mycenae?"

"Well, *I'd* arranged to go to Mycenae with Mr. Blunt, you remember. The night before. And Mr. James heard me talking about it."

"So Henry *was* . . ."

"I'm not sure," Marius said slowly. "I think he believed to the bitter end that Bubi was merely trying to smuggle in whiskey. He clearly didn't know about the balcony, poor devil."

"Poor Henry."

"But, Mrs. Erskine, may I ask you just one thing? How did you manage to get the treasures away from Mary-Lou without her knowing?"

"How? Oh, that was easy. It was in the little girls' room at the airport. She was fixing her face—total concentration required, as you know—and I just took them out of her basket and put them in my bag. She didn't notice a thing. And I put in a few cans of—well, you know, disinfectant—to equalize the weight. But it seems the police were watching us both after all." She smiled briefly.

Lydia looked at her curiously. "But when you'd got the

treasures safely at Athens why did you come on to Lindos with Mary-Lou? You must have known who she was going to meet and that you'd be in danger—*great* danger."

"Oh, honey, I think you're exaggerating there a little . . ." Mrs. Erskine fiddled with her glass.

"They might have killed you."

"Or *you!*"

"You mean," Lydia said slowly, "that you walked deliberately into all that because you were worried about me?"

"Not exactly that . . ."

"And saved my life—"

"Oh, nonsense! I ought to be ashamed of myself. Taking the treasures *with* me up there. Why, anything could have happened to them! I should have put them in a luggage locker or something, but I just never thought of it. Well, anyway, here we all are, safely. Now, I see here"— she was running a finger down the index of her guidebook —"that there are two other *very* interesting sites on Rhodes. Early ones. And I guess as I'm here I ought to see some of the other islands . . ."

Marius cleared his throat. "Lydia and I," he said loudly, "thought that we would stay on in Rhodes for a few days."

"Did we?" For a moment Lydia was genuinely puzzled. Mrs. Erskine was quicker. "*Did* you? Did you really?" Her face broke into a broad enchanting smile. "Oh, I am so pleased!"

"Pleased?"

"I thought you'd approve," Marius said comfortably.

"Of *course* I do! It's just lovely, *and* it solves a problem that's been bothering me. I've been wondering"—she groped in the pocket of her raincoat, which was hanging over the back of her chair—"what to do with this." Carefully she placed a small object on the table in front of Lydia.

There was a moment of silence.

"I do hope you like it," Mrs. Erskine said wistfully.

It was a round cup about four inches high, set on a pedestal in the shape of four lions' paws. Around the bowl itself were four lion faces snarling in defiance. The whole thing gave an impression of grace and—it was the only word for it—of lightheartedness. And it was made of a yellow gold that Lydia and Marius instantly recognized.

Mrs. Erskine said, "I would so much like you two nice young people to have it since you're going to be—together."

Lydia said weakly, "But you can't—the Greek government—"

"They've got so much," Mrs. Erskine said tranquilly. "And Major Papandros meant me to have it, I'm sure. He kind of—let it drop. Please take it. . . . Mr. Erskine doesn't really appreciate antiques."

Lydia said, "Nothing's actually fixed, you know."

"No," agreed Mrs. Erskine, "but—"

"But you'll think about it?" Marius said eagerly.

"Oh, yes, I'll certainly think."

*Foreboding mansions,
moonlight and the moaning wind
... a setting for romance,
intrigue and the supernatural*

GOTHIC MYSTERIES

BELLWOOD   *Elisabeth Ogilvie*   60c

THE BRIDE OF MOAT HOUSE

Peter Curtis   60c

CHATEAU IN THE SHADOWS

Susan Marvin   60c

COME TO CASTLEMOOR   *Beatrice Parker*   75c

THE CRAIGSHAW CURSE   *Jean Francis Webb*   60c

THE DANCER'S DAUGHTER

Josephine Edgar   60c

DUNSAN HOUSE   *Anita Grace*   60c

GIANT'S BREAD   *Mary Westmacott*   60c

THE HERMITAGE   *Mary Kay Simmons*   75c

A HOWLING IN THE WOODS

Velda Johnston   60c

I START COUNTING   *Audrey Erskine Lindop*   75c

THE JACKAL'S HEAD   *Elizabeth Peters*   75c

THE SANDALWOOD FAN

Katherine Wigmore Eyre   75c

TIMBALIER   *Clayton W. Coleman*   60c

WOMAN IN THE MAZE   *Maeva Park Dobner*   60c

DELL BOOKS

If you cannot obtain copies of these titles from your local bookseller, just send the price (plus 15c per copy for handling and postage) to Dell Books, Post Office Box 1000, Pinebrook, N. J. 07058. No postage or handling charge is required on any order of five or more books.

"Extraordinary is the word to be used first, last, and repeatedly about this book . . . . Anyone who meets Karen, even on paper, will postpone resigning from the human race."

—*The Saturday Review*

KAREN 60c
Marie Killilea

As told by her mother, the inspirational story of Karen, who—despite a handicap—learns to talk, to walk, to read, to write. Winner of the Golden Book Award and two Christopher Awards.

WITH LOVE FROM KAREN 60c
Marie Killilea

Written in response to thousands of letters, this sequel to *Karen* tells of her growth from seven years old into womanhood and relates more about the open friendliness and spiritual plenty of her family.

If you cannot obtain copies of these titles from your local bookseller, just send the price (plus 15c per copy for handling and postage) to Dell Books, Post Office Box 1000, Pinebrook, N. J. 07058. No postage or handling charge is required on any order of five or more books.

Now in paperback—the inspiring true story
of how the child who lived a miracle grew up
...*"full of tenderness, pathos,
humor and great courage."*
—New York Journal-American

WITH LOVE
FROM KAREN

by MARIE KILLILEA

The heartwarming sequel to KAREN, written
in response to the more than 27,000 letters
received by Marie Killilea
asking what happened to Karen.

A DELL BOOK   60c